NO MORE SECRETS

JAMEY MOODY

As an independent author, reviews are greatly appreciated.

No More Secrets

©2021 by Jamey Moody. All rights reserved

Edited: Kat Jackson

This is a work of fiction. Names, characters, places, and incidents are the product of the author's imagination or are used fictitiously. Any resemblance to an actual person, living or dead, business establishments, events, or locales is entirely coincidental. This book, or part thereof, may not be reproduced in any form without permission.

Thank you for purchasing my book. I hope you enjoy the story.

If you'd like to stay updated on future releases, you can visit my website or sign up for my mailing list here: www.jameymoodyauthor.com.
I'd love to hear from you! Email me at jameymoodyauthor@gmail.com.

❦ Created with Vellum

ALSO BY JAMEY MOODY

Live This Love

The Your Way Series:

Finding Home

Finding Family

Finding Forever

It Takes A Miracle

One Little Yes

The Lovers Landing Series

Where Secrets Are Safe

No More Secrets

"You felt like you were exactly where you should be. Your soul found its home."

Julia Lansing

1

"Say something!"

"There's nothing to say."

"You've always got something to say," Julia Lansing said, eyeing her best friend.

"Not this time, Jules," Krista Kyle replied, gazing at her beloved lake. It had been three months since that disastrous walk down the aisle; well, more like an almost walk down the aisle.

Before that she'd been living her best life or at least she'd thought she was. Krista was an award winning actress and now producer. The production company she founded, Ten Queens, had produced the biggest blockbuster to date featuring a queer storyline with queer women acting in leading roles. It was more than a movie about gay people in the gay community. It followed queer people in everyday life, living life. Krista was extremely proud of the company and the quality entertainment they were creating.

She had started the company not long after she and Julia had purchased this old run-down lake resort and turned it into the best kept secret in Hollywood. Lovers Landing was the secret hideaway Krista and Julia had created for the closeted queers in high profile careers where being out could harm them professionally. Sadly that was the way the world still worked in some circles, but Lovers Landing was a place they could come and be themselves.

There, women could hold one another's hands without fear it would end up on social media in a matter of minutes. There was a private beach, a restaurant with romantic little nooks for secluded dinners, and a bar with nightly karaoke. Each couple had its own cabin that backed up to the water with gorgeous sunrise or sunset views. It was romantic, peaceful, and more importantly, secluded. Secrets were safe, people were happy, and love flourished.

It was during their inaugural season that everything almost ended before it began. Krista, Julia, and Lovers Landing hosted many happy couples that first summer, but a journalist that made a name by outing lesbian stars heard about the hideaway.

Krista made it her mission to keep this journalist from ruining her and Julia's dreamland for closeted lovers. What she didn't plan on was falling in love with the journalist, but then again does anyone ever plan on falling in love?

Brooke Bell was a talented writer with her own secret when she came to Lovers Landing. Krista was determined to save the resort, but in the process she saved Brooke, too. She helped Brooke see her worth and rewrite her career out of the depths of sleazy sensationalist journalism into an Academy Award winning screenwriter.

They fell in love fast and hard. It was a whirlwind romance and they worked side by side with their other Lovers Landing friends and made the movie they were all now known for. Three months ago on the night they received their Oscars, the group boarded a plane and came to Lovers Landing to celebrate.

Caught up in the success, joy, and love, Krista and Brooke thought it would be a great time for a quick wedding. Their friends would already be there and it would be a fun surprise. Now that Krista looked back on it, she could admit it was her insane idea to get married. Brooke was just going along like she had for the last three years—until she didn't.

Julia reached over and took Krista's hand and squeezed.

"Don't do that Jules, you'll make me cry," Krista said, looking out over the water. "That is, if I had any tears left." Krista chuckled sarcastically. "Ironic, isn't it? I once encouraged Brooke to cry and told her that tears were healing. If that wasn't the biggest line of bullshit!" She shook her head. "All I've done is cry and nothing is healed. So, my dear friend. I don't have anything to say."

"I've tried to be patient with you, Krissy. You've got to talk about it so you can go on."

"Go on? Where am I going, Jules?"

"You haven't been back to LA. You've barely been out of your cabin."

"I've been working. I'm reading scripts for new projects."

"Krista, come on."

Krista sighed. "Look Julia, I've lived it over and over. It was my fault."

"What? Your fault? What do you mean?"

"I knew Brooke lived with considerable guilt over how she treated her first love. I am the dumbass that suggested she contact her. I thought she would see that this woman had a good life and it would ease the guilt."

"You had no way of knowing Brooke was still in love with her," Julia said supportively.

"First love is a mighty strong emotion, isn't it?" Krista smiled sadly at Julia then looked away.

Julia furrowed her brow. "It is. Are you sure you're talking about Brooke?"

"I am," Krista said convincingly. "God, Jules, we were walking down the deck, hand in hand. Brooke Eden's 'Got No Choice' was playing through the sound system. I looked out and could see you and Heidi holding hands, smiling at us. And then Brooke stopped," Krista said, remembering.

"We were remembering our own wedding for a split second when we saw Brooke simply quit walking," Julia recalled.

"She stopped and said, 'I can't do this.'" Krista shook her head. "That really is all that needs to be said, Julia. Brooke reconnected with her first love and will probably live happily ever after with her.

That's it. That's all. I'm not supposed to have a partner. Karma, history or whatever has shown me over and over and this time I get it. I'm listening. I'm done."

"What? No way!"

"Yep, I'm done. I'm fifty-three years old and that's enough. I'm also done talking about this."

Julia started to object but Krista stopped her.

"I mean it, Jules," she said, looking over at her best friend.

Julia looked at her for several moments and then exhaled. "Okay, but you're going to have to help me here this week."

"The last group just left. We have a week off before the next one gets here and then the next week is our Ten Queens meeting. What do you need help with?"

"I know it's our week off, but I'm doing someone a favor," Julia replied.

"A favor?"

"Yes. A family contacted me and wanted to rent out a couple of the cabins."

Krista chuckled. "You explained to them that this isn't exactly a family resort, right?"

"Of course I did, but they were persuasive. Besides, it doesn't hurt to be nice occasionally."

"You're always nice. What did you do, Jules?" Krista asked, narrowing her eyes.

"This family came here years ago, probably when we worked here in high school. They wanted to recreate special memories they had here for their kids. They promised they wouldn't be any trouble. They simply want the cabins and I agreed to let them use the paddle boards."

"What about the restaurant? It will be closed. What about the boats and the bikes?"

"I told them the restaurant would be closed and I gave them access to one boat."

Krista eyed her friend and shook her head. "Why would you do that? Lots of people contact us and don't realize we're not a family resort. You explained it and they still want to come?"

"I told them it was our off-week and they were fine with it."

"Of course they're fine with it. They'll have the place to themselves. I'm not sure this is a good idea, Jules."

"It's done. You wouldn't even know they're here, but turns out I need to be gone Tuesday. I'll check them in tomorrow. All I need you to do is take the boat keys to them Tuesday afternoon."

"Why can't you give them the keys tomorrow?"

"Because the marina has both boats in for service. They picked them up today and will bring them back Tuesday."

Krista stared at Julia, not sure she was getting the whole story. "You'll check them in tomorrow and you need me to take them the keys. That's it?"

Julia nodded. "That's it. I don't know why you're making a big deal. It's not like you've done anything around here the last three months anyway."

Krista jerked back as if Julia had hit her.

"I didn't mean that the way it sounded, Krissy. What I mean is that you haven't been to the office or even the beach in a very long time. You're supposed to be my partner in this place. I've tried to go easy, but I need your help."

"Don't give me that shit. I know Becca has been running this place and doing a fantastic job. She is your daughter and you taught her well. You are not going to make me feel guilty for taking some time to myself."

Julia narrowed her eyes and stared at Krista. "Don't you get it? I miss you! You're my best friend and I barely see you."

Krista softened. "I know, Jules. It's easier to work on these scripts than think about what happened. I couldn't watch all those happy couples holding hands and having fun. It was too much." Krista took Julia's hand and smiled. "I will take care of this family and I will be right beside you when the next group comes in. How's that?"

"You will? They seem really nice."

"I will."

Julia chuckled. "I'd almost like to see their faces when the superstar Krista Kyle brings them their boat keys."

Krista laughed with her. "You haven't called me that since we worked here over thirty years ago."

"I remember those happy times."

"Me too, Jules. Me too."

Krista looked over the water, thinking back to when she was twenty-one and working side by side with Julia at this resort. Her biggest care then was when she could steal another kiss from Melanie Zimmer. Those were the days. Simple and sweet. If only she'd known.

2

The next day Krista came walking into the office with a smile on her face and a spring in her step. "Hey Jules."

Julia looked up, obviously shocked. "What are you doing here?"

"As someone pointed out to me yesterday, I work here," Krista said, picking up a document on her desk.

Julia tilted her head. "That doesn't explain why you're here today."

"Did you get your guests checked in?" Krista asked, looking up at her friend.

"They'll be here shortly. Why?" Julia asked, getting up and coming around her desk.

"In our conversation yesterday you neglected to tell me which cabins they're staying in. I might need that information if I'm supposed to bring them boat keys."

"Oh," Julia said, relaxing her posture. "They're staying in your cabin and my cabin."

Krista looked up from the document she was reading and said, "Our cabins? Why would you put them there?"

"The others weren't ready from the last group and those are the ones they requested if possible. I didn't think you'd mind since you've been staying out at the edge of the property in number five. I still don't know why you did that. Are there too many memories in your cabin?"

"No!" Krista said emphatically. "If I was going to let memories keep me out of that cabin I'd never have renovated it in the first place. You know that's the cabin where Melanie and I began and unfortunately that's where we ended too." Krista realized that it was twice in as many days that her first love's name had come up.

"I don't know about that," murmured Julia.

"I can't help thinking of her this time of year," Krista said wistfully.

"That was a great summer," Julia commented.

"It was one of the best summers of my life," Krista said with a smile. She turned to Julia. "You and Heidi, me and Mel; we had such good times."

Julia nodded and smiled back at her. "Yeah we did."

They both were lost in the memories of that summer when Julia's phone pinged. She reached for it and read the message. "They just came through the gate."

"I'll let you get them checked in," Krista said, walking towards the door. "Hey Jules." She stopped and turned back to Julia. "Why don't you and Heidi come out one night this weekend? I'll cook; we can watch the stars come out."

"We would love that," Julia said, walking to her friend.

Krista put her hands on Julia's shoulders and started to say something but hugged her instead. "Tell the guests to call me if they need anything." Then she let Julia go and walked out of the office and out the back door.

Julia watched her leave and then walked through to the counter just as the front door opened. Two women in their late thirties came in with a young girl and a little boy rubbing the sleep out of his eyes.

Julia's face beamed. "Stephanie Zimmer, I'd know you anywhere."

The taller woman smiled back at Julia and watched her walk around the counter. "Hi Julia!"

Julia hugged her and stepped back. "You look so much like your mother."

"Mom is beautiful, so thanks. Actually, I'm Stephanie Zimmer-Lopez now." She smiled. "I'd like for you to meet my wife, Heather, and these are our kids. Ava is eight and Kyle is five."

Julia shook Heather's hand and said, "It is so nice to meet you." She looked down at both kids and grinned. "Do you like to swim?" she asked.

Ava gave her a shy smile and nodded and Kyle jumped up and said, "Yes!"

Julia laughed. "Then you are going to love it here."

"Ava, Kyle look over here," Heather said, winking at Stephanie. "We can see the lake out the window." Heather led the kids to the huge windows that looked out to the deck and down to the beach and water.

"This looks different, but also familiar from what I remember," said Stephanie.

"We kind of refreshed everything when Krista and I bought it. We've updated and expanded the bar and restaurant and wanted to highlight the big windows with the lake view."

"It's awesome!" Stephanie turned to Julia. "I can't believe I'm here. Thanks so much for helping us make this happen."

"You have no idea how perfect the timing is."

"Was that Krista I glimpsed going out the back door when we came in?"

"Yes. I didn't expect her to be here today. I was afraid she might see you."

"She has no idea then?"

"Nope." Julia grinned and her eyes sparkled mischievously.

"When Heather wanted to do something special for my fortieth birthday I told her about this place and how much I loved it here that summer. I've always wanted to bring the kids here, but whenever I mentioned it to Mom, a sadness would come over her. I never did understand why because we all had such good memories here, you know."

"Oh, I remember. Krista and I were just talking about how wonderful that summer was."

"I happened to be with Mom when I was reading a magazine and saw the story about Krista's break-up with Brooke Bell. I showed it to her and I'll never forget the look on her face. I'm such an idiot, but it finally all made sense then."

"She never said anything to you and Jennifer about that summer?"

"Not about her relationship with Krista. We always thought they were friends. I don't know why they kept it a secret. I mean, Krista was one of Mom's first big clients and we had that connection from the summer. Over the years we've kept in touch even though we didn't get to see each other often. She sent us Christmas and birthday gifts and would call. I haven't seen her since Kyle was born." Stephanie chuckled and continued. "I remember when we found out we were having a boy, I video called Krista and told her I wanted to name him Kyle. You should have seen her face."

"Oh, I remember. She called me as soon as she hung up with you. She was thrilled."

"She's like the other parent that we always knew we could count on even though we didn't get to see her as much as we wanted. I remember that first year on weekends we'd get to come see y'all at your apartment and then when Krista moved to LA and Mom was so busy with work we didn't get to see her. She made up for it with letters at first and then cell phones made it much easier." Stephanie met Julia's eyes and asked, "Julia, do you know what happened between them?"

Julia stared at her and sighed. "I think it was timing. Until now."

Stephanie nodded. "I asked Mom, but she was very cryptic and said she was coming for her heart. I've never seen her that upset. She said this had gone on long enough."

Julia smiled. "It's about fucking time," she said quietly.

Stephanie's eyebrows crept up her forehead. Julia shrugged.

"After Mom read that story things started happening." Stephanie leaned against the counter. "Jennifer and I had been trying to get her to let us take over the business, but she said she wasn't ready. Then all of a sudden she was and started the transition, turning her clients over to us. She talked with Heather and planned this big birthday party for me here and then last week she sold her house."

"What?"

"Yeah. Her house was on the market for three days and boom, it sold."

"Wow!"

Stephanie eyed Julia closely and asked, "But you know some of this, don't you?"

Julia nodded. "I didn't know she'd sold the house. I knew about the business and she called me about coming here." She paused. "Look, Steph, Krista is still very hurt, but she is going to be so happy to see y'all. I'm not sure what you're expecting, but I think your mom wants to surround Krista in your love. Because that is the only thing that can heal her broken heart."

"You see, Julia. That's what I'm wondering. Did my mom break Krista's heart?"

Julia's face softened. "You'll have to ask Krista."

Stephanie nodded. "You know what," she said, looking around the room and then over at her family. "This is where the magic began and I can feel it. It's still here," she said, spreading out her arms. "Once we get them together tomorrow we'll let the magic do the rest."

"I hope you're right," Julia said. "Come on, I'll show you to your cabins."

"Jenny and her family will be here later with Mom."

"I've told Krista to bring the boat keys to you tomorrow afternoon. She's staying over at the last cabin on the property."

"I can't wait to see her. "

Julia smiled and led them out of the building and took them to their cabin. On her way home she thought about what Krista had said last night about karma and not having a partner. Maybe the universe was finally aligned so her best friend could live happily ever after. "Oh I hope so," she said aloud.

3

Krista put her iPad down and sighed. She didn't know why, but she couldn't concentrate on the script she'd been trying to read. Melanie kept creeping into her mind. It was about this time of year when Melanie came into her life. She thought she had found the person she'd be with the rest of her life. Oh she was young, but their connection was something she'd never felt before and hadn't felt since.

She blew out a deep breath and looked around. It wouldn't have surprised her to find Melanie down at the water right outside her cabin. They had always known when the other was near. Krista hadn't had that feeling in a very long time, but then again it had been years since she'd actually been in the same room with Melanie. She got up and looked out the window and laughed at herself. "You're feeling this way because she's been on your mind and it's that time of year, dumbass."

It wasn't quite dark and she figured the guests would be in their cabins so she decided to go for a walk to shake this feeling. She walked along the water past several other cabins that she knew were unoccupied. The moon wasn't quite full and it reflected off the water giving it a shimmering romantic effect. It would be even more beautiful in a few days, she thought, as it waxed to fullness. This made her chuckle; she was never romancing a woman ever again. No thank you.

She looked up as the dock and beach came into view. A quick glance to her left and she could see no lights in the building that housed the restaurant, bar, and their offices. The guard lights were on and she could see the bugs circling the light as darkness fell. A sense of pride filled her knowing she and Julia had indeed turned this place into a haven for women.

A smile was on her face when she looked back over the water and immediately stopped walking. At the end of the dock she saw someone staring at the moon and out over the water. She'd know her anywhere. Krista's heart began to pound rapidly in her chest. And as if she could hear it, the woman turned slowly and looked in Krista's direction.

"Mel?" Krista whispered as she stepped on the walkway and glided toward her as if pulled by an invisible force.

"Kris," Melanie said softly. She held out her arms and Krista walked into them and melted into the embrace.

For a moment everything was right with the world.

Krista pulled back and looked at Melanie, not trusting her eyes. "What are you doing here?"

"I came back to where it all began."

"What began?" Krista asked, confusion laced in her voice.

"You and me. Us."

"Mel," Krista started, but Melanie interrupted her.

"It's time for us to be honest, to say the things we couldn't. Don't you think thirty-two years is long enough?"

All Krista could do was stare. Surely she was in the middle of a dream.

"It's okay," Mel said, putting her hand on Krista's heart like she'd done so many times before. "I know your heart is hurting, but I need something from you, Krista. I need a promise."

"A promise?"

"I need to relive our magical summer. Would you help me do that?"

"I don't understand," Krista said, becoming more and more confused.

"You know I've kept most of our story from the girls," Mel began. Krista nodded. "I'm ready to tell them and I need you to help me do it. Will you help me tell them the parts of that summer they don't remember? Will you tell them our story, just the way it happened, when we fell in love?" She paused and watched Krista's eyes shining in the moonlight. "Then, I want to be honest with you about what happened afterwards. Would you promise to be honest with me? I know I have no right to ask, but I need to do this."

Krista ran her hand through her hair. All she could do was stare at Melanie. She would do anything for Melanie and the girls. That's the way it had always been, but she didn't know if her heart could do this. It was so battered and bruised. To relive those moments would make it happy, but she also knew what came after that summer. Honestly her heart felt better just thinking about Melanie and that strong bond was proving to still be there or at least know when the other was near.

"Are you saying you haven't been honest with me?" Krista finally asked.

"I haven't and neither have you."

Krista's heart began beating wildly in her chest once again.

"I can see the battle going on behind your eyes," Melanie said.

"I'm not sure my heart can take it. That's honesty, Mel."

She nodded. "The girls should hear our story from us."

"Why now?"

"Our time is finally here."

"What?" Krista said skeptically.

Mel had a half smirk, half smile on her face. "Do you trust me? How many times have you asked me that over the years, Krista? Now it's your turn." She raised her eyebrows and challenged Krista with each word. "Do you trust me?"

Krista visibly swallowed. "Yes," she said softly.

Melanie's face softened and she looked at Krista's lips just as squeals and laughter filtered over the water from the woods.

They both turned and could barely make out shadows moving toward the beach.

"Mom?"

"Mimi? Where are you?"

Melanie could see a smile light Krista's face even in the dark.

"I think you've been missed," Krista said as she watched the figures walk closer.

"Do you miss me, Kris?" Melanie asked, suddenly serious.

Krista turned toward Melanie as her smile turned sad. "I always miss you, Mel."

Melanie let out a breath and sighed. "If you only knew." Then she stepped toward the walkway and yelled, "Over here!"

"Is everyone with you?"

"Yep. Come on. They've been waiting to see you."

Krista followed Melanie up the walkway to the shore.

"Oh my God! Krista!" Jennifer said, jumping into her arms. "I didn't think we'd get to see you until tomorrow."

Krista grinned and hugged her tight. "If I would've known you were coming I'd have met you at the office," she said, looking sharply at Melanie.

Melanie shrugged and Jennifer put her hands on her son's shoulders. "Do you remember Mason?"

"Of course I do. Are you going to let me teach you to ski this week?"

"Yes ma'am!"

Krista chuckled as Jennifer said, "She taught me to ski right here." Jennifer turned to her mother. "You wandered off and we got a little worried."

"Sorry. I decided to walk down to the dock." She looked at Krista and said, "Someone else had the same idea."

Krista smiled, but didn't say anything. Deep down she knew Melanie felt that same old feeling she did. For a moment her heart was soothed, but she also wondered what Melanie was really doing here.

"We were going to surprise you tomorrow," Jennifer said, grinning at Krista.

"This is the best surprise I've had—"

"Ever!" Mason said, jumping up and down.

Krista looked down at him and laughed. "You know what, Mason? Yes, this is the best surprise ever!"

"I knew it!" He walked up and put his arms around Krista. "I like talking to you on FaceTime, but it's nice to hug you for real."

Tears welled up in Krista's eyes as she put her arms around the boy's shoulders, his head nestled against her chest. "You give the best hugs, Mason," she said, her voice thick with emotion.

"He sure does," Melanie said, tears in her eyes as well.

"Preston is going to be so mad I got to surprise you first!" Mason said.

"Well, let's go surprise him. What do you say?"

The boy smiled up at her and put his hand in hers. "Let's go!" he said, dragging her towards the trail to their cabins.

They walked off and Krista looked behind her to see Melanie and Jennifer following behind, their faces shining brightly in the moonlight.

4

They walked into the backyard of the cabin and Mason dropped Krista's hand and ran shouting to the others.

"Krista's here! Krista's here!"

"He really knows how to make your heart feel better doesn't he?" Krista said to Jennifer.

"Yeah he does. I can't tell you how often he picked me up during the divorce. Still does. I should have sent him to you when I heard about you and Brooke."

Krista looked over at Jennifer and knew she shared some of the same feelings. She put her arm around her and squeezed her into her side.

"Hey!" Stephanie said, running up and grabbing Krista. "I missed you so much!"

Krista hugged her tightly. She had to swallow her emotions before they overwhelmed her. "I had no idea how much I'd missed you all until this moment. Whew," she said, looking around at the group of people she loved so very much.

"Mason said you're teaching him how to ski tomorrow. Will you teach me too?" asked Preston.

"I will for a hug," Krista said, teasing him.

He immediately stepped up and put his arms around her middle. "Shit, when did you get so tall?" she said, astonished.

"Krista said a bad word." Ava giggled.

"That's my Krista," Melanie murmured.

Krista looked over the top of Preston's head and her eyes met Melanie's. For a moment, seeing how Melanie looked at her with such love, she was swept back thirty-two years.

"She sounds like your mom, Ava," Jennifer said playfully.

"Very funny. Your Aunt Jennifer talks the same way."

"Come here, Ava. Let me see how big you are before I say another bad word," Krista said.

Ava walked over and hugged Krista.

"How about me?" Kyle said, sticking out his chest. "I'm big now, too!"

"You sure are," Krista said, walking over and picking him up. "And heavy too!"

Kyle grinned and hugged her neck.

She put him down and said, "Okay, line up, you little Zimmers." She put her hand up and said, "Before you say Zimmer isn't your last name, I know that, boys. But you're still Zimmers."

The kids lined up and Krista looked them over. "Okay, here goes. Preston, you're eleven and Mason, you're nine. That would make Ava eight and you sir," she said looking down at Kyle, "you can't be five already!"

"I sure am!" he said, holding up his hand and splaying his fingers indicating how old he was.

Krista shook her head at the kids and then saw Heather standing behind them smiling.

"I was wondering about you," Krista said, walking over to hug her.

"You had quite a few Zimmers to get through first," Heather said, grinning.

"Now, would someone please tell me what y'all are doing here! Julia said it was a family that came here years ago. She kept your secret."

Stephanie and Jennifer looked at Melanie and then at Krista.

"The summer we spent here with you shaped our lives and we wanted our kids to see this place, but more importantly we wanted to see you," said Stephanie.

"Did you know that I created this place around the things we did and the things that happened that summer?" Krista smiled. "You can thank your Mom that we're even here because she made me tons of money so Julia and I could buy this place."

"We remember things about that summer, but Mom said there's a lot more to it and she's finally agreed to tell us with your help. Will you tell us how the Zimmer-Kyles began?" said Jennifer.

Krista could feel tears stinging her eyes and when she looked at Melanie she saw tears pooled in her eyes as well. "The Zimmer-Kyles," Krista said, chuckling. "Is that what we are?"

"Aren't we a family?" Stephanie asked.

Krista smiled and nodded. "Yeah we are."

"It's kind of late to start this tonight," Melanie said, speaking up.

"We can't really tell it without our costars, can we?" Krista said.

A smile grew on Melanie's face. "Julia and Heidi?"

"Exactly. How about we all have dinner in the restaurant tomorrow night?"

"I thought it was closed," said Stephanie.

"It is, but I know the owner." Krista winked.

They all laughed.

"We can grill burgers and hot dogs and eat on the deck," said Krista.

"Just like we did at your parents' house," said Jennifer excitedly.

"You remember that?" Krista asked, surprised.

"Of course we do. Your parents were so much fun. They had that cool swing set in the back yard and your mom went to the city pool with us," said Stephanie.

"It was like having another set of grandparents," Jennifer said, laughing.

"I can't believe you remember that."

"I told you. That summer was special. What I remember most is love. We were so loved," said Stephanie.

"Yeah and to think, we didn't want to come in the first place," Jennifer said, chuckling. "And when we met you that very first day and you took us riding in that golf cart, we knew everything was going to be all right."

"Oh you did not!" exclaimed Krista.

"Yes we did!" Stephanie and Jennifer said together.

"Besides, they're our memories," said Stephanie, protectively.

Krista shook her head and chuckled. "Okay, okay." She looked at Melanie. "I'll call Julia and see if she and Heidi can come. She supposedly was busy tomorrow so I had to help out here. I'm beginning to think she was fooling me." She turned to the kids and said, "What do y'all think? Was she teasing me?"

They all laughed. "She was." Ava giggled. "I heard her when we checked in."

"I'm not going to be mad at her because y'all are the best surprise EVER!" she said, grinning at Mason.

"Yeah we are!" he agreed.

"How about I come get you in the morning and I'll teach you how to paddle board. The boats won't be ready until tomorrow afternoon. I'll teach you to ski then."

"Yes!" the kids said, jumping up and down.

"That sounds perfect," said Heather.

"Okay then. It's kind of late. Y'all had better get to bed so you'll be ready for tomorrow."

"Good idea. Come on kids," Heather said, leading them inside.

"I'll see you in the morning," Jennifer said, hugging Krista and following the kids.

Stephanie hugged her. "I'm so glad to see you."

"I'm happy you're here."

She smiled and joined the others.

Melanie looked carefully at Krista. "Are you happy?" Melanie asked.

"What?"

"Are you happy we're here?"

"Yes," Krista breathed.

"I'll take care of your heart," Melanie declared.

"Mel..."

"Come on," Melanie said, hooking her arm in Krista's. "I'll walk you to your cabin."

"You can walk me to the beach. I don't want you getting lost on the way back."

"I can't get lost, Kris. I'm here with you."

They walked in silence until Krista stopped them. "You go back now. I'll be fine."

"Why aren't you living in our cabin? I know it's yours; I could feel you when I walked inside it."

"I needed to be away from everyone. The cabin I'm in is out of the way."

Melanie nodded and looked into Krista's eyes. She cupped the side of Krista's face and said softly, "I'll see you in the morning."

Krista watched her walk away and sighed. She couldn't help but wonder, as she had so many times, what would've happened if she hadn't listened to Melanie Zimmer all those years ago.

When she got back to her cabin she called Julia.

"Hey, I'm not going to be able to deliver those boat keys tomorrow," she said when Julia answered.

"Why not? Krista you have to," Julia said firmly.

"You will never guess who I ran into tonight when I walked over to the dock."

There was silence on the line.

"Come on Julia. Don't you want to guess," Krista baited her.

"Uh," Julia stammered.

Krista laughed. "Would you do something for me?"

"Maybe," Julia said tentatively.

"Would you tell me why Melanie is here?"

"Well," Julia began.

"Hold up. I saw her on the dock in the moonlight and I thought my eyes were playing tricks on me, but the reason for the walk was because I couldn't get her off my mind. I could sense that she was near, Julia. I haven't felt that particular feeling in such a long time."

"Is that a bad thing?"

"No. I always miss Mel. Do you know why she's here?"

"She said it was time to tell the girls your whole story and she needed you to help her do that. She said it was your time."

Krista nodded slowly. "She said that on the dock."

"What did you say?"

"I asked her why now? Why she wanted the girls to know. I mean, why does it matter?"

"I think Melanie has kept you as her secret all these years and she doesn't want to anymore."

"Oh Jules." Krista sighed. "I told her I'd tell the story of that summer with her, but I don't think my heart can do any more than that. When I left her tonight, she said she'd take care of my heart. After all we've been through, she says something like that!"

"There has been a big change with her and the girls. Stephanie mentioned it today. I'm sure Melanie will tell you all about it. How was it seeing them? It's been a long time since all of you have been together."

"I didn't realize how much I missed them. Did you see the kids? They're so big! And I could see Jennifer had been through some of the same things I have with her divorce and all."

"Can I make a suggestion?"

Krista chuckled. "When have you ever asked?"

"That's true." Julia laughed. "Why don't you let them wrap you in love and forget about everything this week."

"The last time I did that was when Brooke was here and we know how that turned out," Krista said, the happiness in her voice gone.

"This is different. They are your family and they love you. You can trust them."

Krista chuckled. "Have you been talking to Mel? That's exactly what she asked me—to trust her"

"I remember you asking her that all the time!"

"I did, didn't I?" Krista sighed into the phone.

"What are you afraid of, Krissy? This is Melanie."

"Do you not remember everything after our summer?"

"Of course I do. Y'all had hard choices to make and you did the best you could. And now, your family is right here."

"I'm not so sure reliving the past is a good thing. Stephanie and Jennifer will undoubtedly not agree with the choices we made."

"Doesn't matter. At least they will know why."

"I told them we couldn't tell the story without you and Heidi. We're paddle boarding and skiing tomorrow and then cooking burgers and hot dogs on the deck. Can you come? I'm thinking you're not really busy tomorrow."

Julia laughed. "Of course we'll be there."

"I don't care what you say, Julia. Melanie and I made our decision long ago. She's feeling the nostalgia of being back here. There is no way I will risk this family and where Melanie and I finally are. I'm telling you this now because I know what you're going to say."

"Oh you do, huh? Here's what I have to say, let your family love you. That's it."

"That's it? I'm not sure I believe you, but okay. See you tomorrow."

Krista turned the lights off and looked out her back door. She could see the moonlight reflecting off the water. For a moment she was back on the dock and could feel Melanie's arms around her. When she was in Melanie's arms she always felt safe and at home. After all these years, that hadn't changed. It didn't surprise her, but over the years she would relish when that happened because she knew it was just a moment and they couldn't really be together and share a life like she wanted.

Julia's words rang in her ears: *let your family love you*. She wanted this desperately, but the problem was her family would leave. They always did.

5

Melanie's head was resting on her hands as she stared up at the ceiling. Her eyes roamed around the room and she exhaled. The walls may have had fresh paint and the bed and furniture were different, but she could still feel Krista in this room. She could feel *them*. It was where they fell in love, where her soul found the one it loved. They both felt it that night and it had been that way ever since. It didn't matter that they'd both had other lovers, their souls belonged together.

They always tried to do the right thing for everyone concerned because life was more than just the two of them and they knew that. Why did it have to be so hard for them? Why did they have to make it so hard? Their souls knew and it was time they listened to them. Melanie had finally come to this realization and was doing something about it. She knew it would be hard work to convince Krista, for she had suffered most of all. But she wasn't leaving Krista this time. She wasn't leaving her ever again.

She had a plan. It began by surrounding her with the people she loved most and then an apology. After that she would do what Krista did best, *romance*. She remembered Krista telling her that she made her want to be romantic. Well, it was her turn. They were never too old to be adored, worshipped and romanced. That's exactly what she intended to do.

*　*　*

The laughter wafting up from the beach reached Krista and Melanie where they sat in the adirondack chairs.

"You always were a great teacher," Melanie said as she watched her children and grandchildren paddle board.

"Look at them go." Krista laughed. "Watch out, Mason!" she yelled as he fell into the water followed by a fresh chorus of laughs. "Look at him, Mel," she said, watching the paddlers in the water. "Watch him help Kyle. He's so good with him. What a big heart."

Melanie had been watching Krista as the kids played. Her face was enchanted and lit up with every new fall or success.

"Why are you watching me instead of the kids?" Krista said, glancing over at Melanie with happiness all over her face.

"Because you're beautiful. Do you have any idea how your face lights up when you look at our kids and grandkids."

Krista looked back at her. "Our?"

"Yes, our," Melanie said, pinning her with a look. "You helped raise them more than you know."

Krista didn't say anything.

"You never did promise me last night," Melanie said.

Krista looked over at her and said, "You never told me what you wanted. I agreed to tell our story to the girls. What else do you want?"

"I told you. Honesty."

Krista sighed. "Ah yes. What exactly do you think I kept from you, Melanie?"

"How you really felt. I don't think either of us was honest. I think we were both afraid."

"I'm not sure when you're talking about, Mel. Was it the year after we fell in love, or ten years later? Twenty? We seemed to go in ten year cycles."

"All of it. The promise I want is that you'll be honest with me after we tell the story and it's just you and me. Because I promise you right now, Krista, I will be honest with you the rest of our lives. No more secrets. No more unsaid things that should be spoken."

Krista's eyes had been focused on Melanie's and now they softened. She reached over and smoothed the wrinkle between Melanie's brow. "That little furrow always appears when you're serious. Let's enjoy this day, Mel. These beautiful kids and grandkids are serenading us with laughter and joy. Isn't that why you're here? Let's relive that joy."

Melanie exhaled and her posture relaxed; a smile played at the corners of her mouth. "You were the one that was so serious before."

"And you were the one that taught me to live in the now."

"Did it work?"

Krista smiled. "It does when I'm with you. I learned to savor those moments because we never knew when we'd be together again."

Melanie looked at Krista and could see that twenty-one year old woman smiling back at her.

"I love you, Mel. I hope you haven't forgotten that."

"I haven't. I love you, too."

Krista got up and held out her hand. "Let's go paddle boarding with these awesome people you call ours."

Melanie took her hand and grinned.

"Mimi! Come swim with me!" yelled Ava.

"Kwista! Come paddle with me!" said Kyle.

They looked at one another then joined their family.

***

Later that evening they were gathered around the tables on the deck eating hamburgers and hot dogs. The kids were telling Julia and Heidi all about learning to ski, complete with the best wipe-outs.

"You should have seen Mom and Aunt Stephanie skiing together. It was so cool," Preston explained, full of excitement. "Tomorrow Mason and I are going to try to ski together."

Krista looked on with her face full of joy, watching these kids she loved so much talking so animatedly to her best friend. She took a deep breath and noticed her heart felt full and this time it wasn't accompanied by an ache that she thought would always be there. Maybe Julia was right. She needed to let her family love her. She caught Melanie's eye and said, "Let's make a fire in the fire pit at your cabin. The kids can watch a movie inside while we tell the story."

"You mean your cabin and our story," Melanie said.

This got Julia and Heidi's attention and they both looked on with raised brows.

Krista looked at Melanie as her anxiety level continued to climb. They'd had a good day together. She didn't know when she'd been this happy. It'd been such a long time. But as the moment approached for this big story-telling event she'd become more and more anxious.

As if reading her thoughts Melanie said, "It'll be all right. We'll be all right."

Krista exhaled and nodded. She always felt safe with Melanie, but their time together always ended and it got harder and harder each time. So much so that they hadn't seen one another in a long time. It had taken years, but to protect her heart Krista had made herself think of Melanie as a friend, not her first love, not, if she was honest, her true love—just her friend. Her soul knew differently and she tried to ignore it as she had for the last thirty-two years. There was always some reason they couldn't be together, so she'd become good at ignoring and that too had protected her heart.

"Your cabin looks a lot different than it did thirty years ago, doesn't it Melanie?" asked Julia.

"You know, it does and it doesn't. It is certainly a lot nicer, but some things will never change," she said, looking over at Krista. "I can still remember making you pimento cheese sandwiches for lunch."

Krista looked at Melanie affectionately. "I remember that."

"I remember that too, now that you brought it up," Stephanie said. "Oh, how I looked up to you and I remember trying pimento cheese. There's no way I would have tasted it if Mom suggested it, but when I saw you eat it I had to try." Stephanie chuckled.

Julia laughed. "I remember both of you always wanted to help us when we gathered trash on the beach."

"I know," exclaimed Melanie. "I couldn't get them to pick up anything in their bedroom, but they were always quick to help y'all."

Krista and Julia shared a look and grinned.

"What I remember is that we never felt like you didn't want us around. I know we had to be the biggest pains in your ass," said Jennifer.

"No you weren't! We loved having you with us," said Krista. "I remember one day Julia told me that she wanted to have two little girls just like you. And she was naming the first one Courtney," Krista said, giggling.

"Oh really," said Heidi.

"Yes! And when I asked her what she was naming the other one she said she'd let you name her," Krista explained.

"It was only fair," said Julia, shrugging.

"Did you really say that?" asked Stephanie.

Julia smiled. "I really did and you'll get to meet Courtney and Becca this weekend because they'll both be here."

"Wow," said Jennifer, looking over at her sister. "We must not have been as bad as I thought."

"I wouldn't go that far," deadpanned Julia. "You had your moments."

They all laughed.

"Who wants ice cream?" asked Melanie.

She was met with a chorus of 'me!' Krista and Melanie jumped up and went inside to get the ice cream.

"This has been the best day," said Krista, opening the freezer and getting out the ice cream. "There's a tray of toppings on the counter so they can each create their own."

Melanie got the tray and blocked the doorway into the hall, waiting on Krista.

"What?" Krista said, when Melanie stood and stared.

"I'm just looking," she said with love shining in her eyes. "I know we've been doing this for over thirty years, but when I look at you, Krissy, I'm back in 1991. I don't see the gray in our hair or the wrinkles. I see the wonder, excitement, and love."

Krista smiled at her. "You always did need glasses," she joked. Then she sobered and added, "I see the wrinkles and can't keep from thinking about missed opportunities, Mel. But I always feel your love."

"I know you're wondering why I think it's so important to tell the girls about us and I don't really have an answer for you. Maybe I'm hoping that this time we'll get it right."

"Lord knows we've fucked it up every other time, haven't we?"

"Not every time. There was a first."

They stared at one another and Krista could feel that familiar pull; their souls were at it again. *Just give in*, she thought.

"Do y'all need help?" Julia yelled from the back door.

The moment slipped away and Melanie turned to walk out of the kitchen. "Here we come."

They set the treats down and let each person make their own ice cream sundae. Krista helped Kyle with his and they sat together sharing their desserts.

When everyone was finished they quickly cleaned up and walked over to the cabins where they were staying. Julia, Heidi, and Melanie started building the fire while Stephanie and Jennifer took the kids inside. Krista was walking Ava to the back door when Heather came out of the cabin.

"Mommy is getting the movie started; you'd better hurry," Heather said to her daughter.

"Are you going to be out here telling ghost stories while we watch the movie?" asked Ava, looking from Krista to Heather.

"No ghost stories!" Krista told her. "I'll get scared, Ava."

"You don't have to be scared. Mimi will protect you," Ava told Krista.

"She will?" Krista said, her brow raised.

"Yeah, I heard Mommy say that Mimi protected you. Right Momma?"

Krista looked at Heather.

Heather paused and then realization crossed her face. "Oh, I think I know what you're talking about. Were you listening to us when you were supposed to be reading?"

"No, I heard Mommy say that when I went to get a drink."

Heather nodded and narrowed her eyes. "Okay, but we've talked about eavesdropping."

"I know, Momma. I promise I wasn't doing that," Ava said seriously.

"You'd better get inside before those boys eat all the popcorn," Heather said.

"Have fun, sweetie," Krista said.

Ava wrapped her arms around Krista's middle and gave her a quick hug. "Don't be scared," she said and ran to the back door.

Krista watched her disappear inside and then looked at Heather with her eyebrows raised.

"Uh, Steph saw the story about your split from Brooke in *People* magazine," Heather explained. "Melanie happened to be at the house when she read it. Steph showed it to her and said the look on Melanie's face explained a lot of things she'd been wondering about, like if the two of you were more than friends."

"And?"

"We were discussing it later and Steph mentioned that Melanie was a big activist for equal rights when she first came out."

"She was, still is. There was no way anyone was going to discriminate against her baby because she was gay," Krista said proudly.

Heather smiled. "Steph remembered that when Melanie became so involved with gay rights that it seemed like she distanced herself from you because you hadn't come out yet."

"In a way that's true," Krista said thoughtfully. "But there was more to it."

"I think what Ava overheard was when Steph wondered if

Melanie distanced herself to protect you. So naturally, Ava would think that her Mimi would protect you from anything."

Krista nodded, but before she could say anything Julia walked up and put her arm around her shoulder.

"Are you ready, Krissy?" She grinned.

They started walking over to the fire pit and Julia added, "Let's go back to when we were young and full of hope."

"Do you not still have hope?" Heather asked.

"We always have hope. Right, Krissy?" Julia said, eyeing her best friend.

Krista didn't answer as she walked over and stood next to Melanie. "You're sure about this?" she asked.

Melanie smiled, nodded and took Krista's hand. "Yes, I want them to know about our love."

Krista looked over at Stephanie and Jennifer and there was love but also curiosity on their faces.

"I get to start this never-ending love story," Julia said boldly.

Krista and Melanie looked at her in surprise.

"That's what you always called it, Melanie," Heidi said. "You said and I quote, 'Krista and I have a never-ending love story.'"

Krista looked into Melanie's eyes and they were whisked back to 1991.

"If a June night could talk, it would probably boast it invented romance."
Bern Williams

1991

"Hey, Superstar!"

Krista Kyle shook her head, dislodging the daydream of accepting the Academy Award for Best Actress, and turned to see her best friend Julia Lansing waving at her.

"You have a new guest. Come on!" Julia yelled.

Krista jumped into the golf cart at the edge of the beach and drove toward Julia and the office of Bailey's Camp on the Lake. She and Julia had worked there every summer since the start of high school. In three months they'd start their final year of college and be on their way to dream careers after that.

They were both twenty-one, tan, and full of summer fun. This job was perfect. They could see their friends that came down to the beach, take guests on boat rides on the lake, and at night they could now drink legally in the bar and restaurant.

Bailey's, as it was known on the lake and in town, was a group of cabins that were for rent by the week, weekend, or for the whole summer. There was a restaurant, a bar, a beach, a dock with a couple of boats for rent, and hiking trails. It wasn't as swanky as a resort, but was a seasonal little piece of paradise on a lake in North Texas.

Krista and Julia had grown up in town, ten minutes from the lake, but all the kids came to the lake no matter the season for fun and escape. Little did they know that thirty years from now they'd not only own Bailey's, but Krista indeed would be bringing an Oscar along with several other awards to what would be called Lovers Landing.

Krista pulled up to the office just as a woman and two young girls walked out of the door.

"Hi," Krista said with a big smile on her face. "I'll be happy to show you to your cabin."

"Hi." The woman smiled brightly. "We'd appreciate that."

"I can't wait to swim," the younger girl said excitedly.

"Let's get settled in our cabin first."

"Where are you parked?" Krista asked. "You can follow me to your cabin. Do you want to ride with me?" she asked the girls with a quick smile.

"Mom, can we?"

Their mom grinned at them both. "Okay." She gave Krista an appreciative look.

"I'm Krista," she said, introducing herself.

"Hi Krista, I'm Melanie and these excited gigglers are Stephanie and Jennifer," she said, her eyes sparkling.

"This is Julia," Krista said, nodding at her friend. "If you need anything just ask."

"Hi!" Jennifer said. "Can you take us on a boat ride?"

"Dang, Jenny, you heard Mom. We have to go to the cabin first," said Stephanie, rolling her eyes.

"Let's get your stuff unloaded and then I'll answer all your questions." Krista grinned.

She got in the golf cart and Jennifer and Stephanie followed her. They waited until Melanie started the car then Krista took off toward the water.

"Look at that water!" said Jennifer. "Let's go swimming, Steph."

Krista laughed. "You'll love it here. Bailey's is the perfect place for a summer vacation."

"We're staying all summer!" said Jennifer. "Well, Mom is. Steph and I are going to visit our dad for part of it, but we'll be back."

"Cool," said Krista. "Your cabin has a little beach right out the back door."

"Really?" said Stephanie. "Our own beach!"

Krista smiled and thought about how much fun these two young girls were going to have here. She pulled up to their cabin and watched as Melanie parked the car next to them.

Krista walked around the car. "Do you have your key? I'll show you around and then help you unload."

"It's right here," Melanie said, holding it out to Krista.

When Krista reached for it Melanie almost dropped it and Krista grabbed the key and Melanie's hand.

"Oops," Krista said. She held Melanie's hand in hers for a moment and felt a spark fly up her arm. Their eyes met and Krista's heart began to pound.

"Sorry about that. I can be clumsy," Melanie said with a soft smile.

Krista dropped her hand and returned the smile. "I've got you—I mean the key," she said, her eyes widening.

"Mom, look!" Jennifer yelled.

"I'd better, uh–" Melanie stammered, pointing to the girls.

Krista grinned. "Come on, I think she's found your beach."

They walked around the car and sure enough Jennifer had run

the short distance to where the grass ended and the sand began. Just beyond that the water lapped in small ripples inviting them to come in. Stephanie kicked her flip flops off and walked a few steps into the water.

"This feels so good!" she said.

Jennifer followed her sister. "Can you believe it? Our own beach!"

Krista and Melanie walked up. "I think they like it," Krista said.

"Thank goodness," Melanie said, watching her daughters. Krista looked over with a furrowed brow and Melanie explained. "They liked the idea of coming here; just not all summer."

"Oh, didn't want to leave their friends?"

"Exactly. But this looks great," she said, gazing around the water and the property.

"This is my favorite cabin," Krista said, following her gaze.

"Let's go look inside, girls," said Melanie.

Krista walked up on the porch and unlocked the back door. "Right this way," she said, stepping inside and holding the door for them.

They walked into the living area which opened into a small kitchen. The girls ran down a short hallway and Stephanie came back quickly and said, "There are only two bedrooms."

"I'm sure you'd like to have your own room," said Krista. "But honestly you won't be in there much."

"What do you mean?" asked Stephanie.

"You've got a lake, and a beach, and an awesome back porch, plus all these trees to sit under. We have bikes so you can roam to the restaurant for a Coke or ride to the bigger beach. There are lots of things to do. Have you ever been fishing?"

"No," Stephanie said, turning up her nose.

"I want to," said Jennifer, jumping up and down.

Krista chuckled. "Have you ever been water skiing? I'll teach you."

"You will?" Stephanie asked, now interested.

"I sure will." Krista could feel Melanie watching her interact with the girls and she noticed a smile appear on her face.

"Let's unload the car. I'm sure Krista has other things to do," Melanie said to the girls.

Krista turned to her. "Not at all. I'm here to help. I'd much rather be doing this."

"What else do you have to do?" asked Jennifer as they walked to the car.

"Pick up trash on the beach. So y'all help me out and throw your trash in the cans."

"We will," said Stephanie.

"Did I say something funny?" Krista asked, looking over at Melanie, who had just laughed, as the girls went ahead.

"If I suggested anything like that it would go in one ear and out the other."

"Of course it would," Krista chuckled.

They all grabbed suitcases and bags along with a few grocery sacks and carried them inside the cabin.

"We stopped at the grocery store to get a few things. I didn't know if there would be a place nearby," Melanie said, putting the sacks on the kitchen counter.

Krista looked in the sack she carried and put in on the counter next to the refrigerator and began to unpack it. "You passed a convenience store before the road to our place. They have a few things, but they're expensive. I live in town and would be happy to pick up anything for you and bring it the next day. All you have to do is ask."

"That's really nice of you, Krista," Melanie said, looking over at her. "Do you do that for all your guests?"

"No, but I would for you." Krista grinned and then added, "And the girls."

They stared at one another for a moment until Stephanie walked in from the living area. "Mom, is it okay if I walk down to the beach?"

"Have you unpacked?" Melanie said, tearing her eyes away from Krista.

"Some."

"Let's unpack and then we'll all walk down together. It's not long until dinner."

"Are you eating at the restaurant tonight?" Krista asked.

"Yes. I knew I wouldn't want to cook after driving up today."

"Well, I'll leave so you can get settled. Do you need anything else?"

"Will we see you later?" Jennifer said, walking into the kitchen.

Krista smiled. "Maybe. I'm meeting a few friends here after work."

"Can we go for that boat ride tomorrow?" Jennifer asked.

"We sure can," Krista said and then looked over at Melanie. "I mean, if your mom doesn't have something else planned for you."

Melanie smiled at her. "That's fine. Have fun with your friends."

"Thanks. I'll come by tomorrow."

Melanie nodded and Krista walked to the door smiling to herself. "Bye," she said, turning to give them a wave.

"Thanks for everything, Krista," Melanie said.

"My pleasure," she said and walked out the door.

Krista took a deep breath as she walked to the golf cart. Her stomach was still fluttering from being around Melanie. She had a feeling this was going to be a great summer.

7

Julia walked up to where Krista was sitting on the dock dangling her feet into the water. When she didn't look up she said, "Hello. Earth to Krissy."

"Hey," Krista said as Julia sat down beside her.

"I can't believe you're not out in the boat or off hiking with Melanie and the girls," Julia said, flipping water over at Krista.

"Very funny."

"I don't mean anything by it. You have to admit you've spent a lot of time with them since they got here."

"Isn't that our job? But you're right. I like them. It's been fun teaching the girls to ski. You should have seen their faces when we rode bikes over to the secret beach yesterday," Krista grinned.

"Be careful, Krissy. Don't fall in love with Melanie and those girls."

"What? Fall in love?"

"You can't see how your face lights up when you talk about them. I don't want you to get your heart broken. That's all."

"Jules, I don't even know if she's into women. We haven't really talked about it."

"She'd be crazy not to want a summer fling with you. Trust me, I've been around you both and she's interested."

"How can you be so sure?"

"Are you kidding me? You know it, too. She watches you when you aren't looking. Just be careful because Mrs. Bailey wouldn't like you being quite that friendly with the guests."

Krista smiled and sighed.

"There's a party at David's cabin tonight. Are you going?" asked Julia.

"No. Are you?"

"Heidi's coming in tonight."

"Oh that's right, so now who's having a summer fling? Isn't it interesting that for such a busy law student Heidi has time to come see you for the weekend?"

"I can't help it if she misses me," Julia said, giggling.

Krista bumped her shoulder to Julia's and chuckled. "I'm happy for you, Jules."

"What are you doing tonight if you aren't going to David's? Want to come with us?"

"No thanks. Melanie took the girls to meet their dad. It's his weekend. I thought I'd go by her cabin when I get off and see if she's doing okay. She seemed a little sad when she told me about it yesterday."

"Uh-huh. No girls. Just you and Melanie alone," Julia said suggestively.

Krista looked over at her. "Just what do you think you and Heidi will get up to tonight, Jules? Huh?"

A smirk grew on Julia's face. "I hope we all have a good night."

Krista chuckled and then their attention was drawn to a car that came down from the restaurant and turned onto the road alongside the beach.

"Looks like Melanie made it back," said Julia.

"Yep," Krista said, getting up. "Tell Heidi hello." They started walking back up to the office.

"You'll see us tomorrow. She wants to go boating if they aren't booked up. Thanks again for working for me."

"I'm happy to do it."

"Have fun tonight," said Julia.

"You too."

They quickly grabbed their things and checked out for the day. Julia left and went home to wait on Heidi and Krista bought a six pack of beer to take with her to Melanie's cabin.

She pulled up next to Melanie's car and when she got out she could see Melanie sitting in one of the chairs down at the little beach.

"Hey," she said quietly as she walked to Melanie.

"Hi," Melanie said, looking up at Krista with a big smile. "I'm so glad to see you."

Krista looked down shyly. "You are? I'm glad to see you, too."

"What do you have there?" Melanie asked, looking at the beer in Krista's hand.

"I thought you might want a drink, so I brought beer. I would have brought wine, but I know absolutely nothing about it," Krista said, rambling.

"Beer is good. That's really kind of you."

"I thought you might be a little lonely without the girls," Krista said, handing her a beer.

"Are you going to sit down?" Melanie nodded toward the chair next to her. "What makes you think I wouldn't like the peace and quiet without the girls?"

"Oh," Krista said, sitting down and opening a beer. "I didn't think about that. I can go," she said nervously.

"I'm just kidding," Melanie said, reaching over and covering Krista's hand with her own and giving it a squeeze. "I don't want you to go. I'm glad you're here."

Krista smiled and took a drink of her beer.

"I would think a beautiful young woman like you might be out with friends on a Friday night, though. You haven't mentioned a boyfriend," said Melanie, quirking her eyebrow.

"I haven't, but I thought I was out with a friend tonight," Krista said, pinning Melanie with a heated look.

Melanie swallowed, but didn't look away. "I'd love to be your friend, Krista."

Krista sat back and released a breath as her heart went back into her chest. She took another drink of her beer and Melanie put her hand back over hers again.

"Do you have a boyfriend?" she asked.

Krista smiled. "No."

"Do you have a girlfriend?" Melanie asked as she curled her fingers around Krista's hand.

"No," Krista said.

Melanie quickly looked up into Krista's eyes.

"Well, I hope to," she said smiling and turning her hand over to link her fingers through Melanie's. "Have you ever had a girlfriend?"

Melanie smiled as she looked down at their hands. "It was so long ago; back when I was in college. She wasn't my girlfriend. It wasn't like that back then."

"Back then! It wasn't that long ago, Mel," Krista said kindly.

"A lot has changed in twelve years, Krista. I know it's 1991, but in 1979 when I was twenty-one, you had to be careful."

"I get it. I'm not out and proud or anything like that. Julia and I have a group of friends that look out for one another."

"Are you and Julia..."

"We are best friends and have been since we were in kindergarten. But I've never thought of her that way. We were even afraid to tell one another," she said, chuckling. "When we realized we were both crazy about women it was such a relief. We had someone else to confide in and someone that understood."

"But still you don't have a girlfriend?" asked Melanie.

"Why do you sound so surprised?"

"Because if I was in college with you, honey, you'd be my girlfriend," Melanie said confidently.

"I would, huh." Krista grinned. That not only made her heart beat faster, but made it happy too.

"As nice as it is out here... would you want to go inside?" Melanie asked.

"There is something I'd like to do when it gets dark," said Krista.

Melanie raised her eyebrows. "What's that?"

"Do you trust me?"

"Yes. I've trusted you with my kids, and myself, since we got here."

"Okay then. When it gets dark I have a surprise for you."

Melanie studied Krista as she got up, grabbing the beer and tugging at her hand. They strolled up to the cabin hand in hand. Krista felt so bold holding Melanie's hand out in the open. When they reached the back door Krista stopped and waited as Melanie turned toward her.

"I really want to kiss you," Krista said, stepping in closer.

Melanie looked down at Krista's lips and then into her deep blue eyes. She raised her hand and ran her thumb along Krista's cheek. Ever so slowly she closed the distance between their lips. Her eyes fluttered shut as she touched her lips to Krista's.

Krista could hear her heart beating in her ears and feel it in her chest. She lost her breath when Melanie's lips touched hers. They were soft and warm and felt like they always belonged pressed to hers. A small moan hummed through Krista's throat.

Melanie pulled away slightly with a small smile, her fingers firmly holding the side of Krista's neck. "Let's go inside," she whispered. Then, looking into Krista's eyes, she quickly kissed her again. She reached for the door and opened it.

Krista let out a breath and walked in, quickly putting the beer in the refrigerator. When she turned around Melanie was at the opposite counter. In one step Krista put her arms around Melanie's neck and pulled her down for a kiss.

It began soft and sensual and a bit tentative, but Krista wanted those lips against hers from now on. She tightened her arms, pulling Melanie closer, and then ran her tongue over Melanie's bottom lip. She heard Melanie moan and then she opened her mouth, inviting Krista's tongue inside. When their tongues met it was Krista's turn to moan.

She explored Melanie's mouth and was suddenly aware of their chests pressed tightly together. That's when Melanie pushed her tongue past Krista's lips and they both moaned again. Their tongues danced and stroked and tasted until they both had to breathe.

Melanie rested her forehead against Krista's and chuckled. "This is not where I imagined I'd be kissing you."

Krista leaned back so she could see into Melanie's brown eyes. "You've imagined kissing me?" she said, delighted.

Melanie looked down, a grin playing at the corners of her mouth. Then she looked back into Krista's sparkling eyes. "I did and this was so much better than I imagined."

Krista smiled, then tilted her head. "Maybe we should do it again to be sure."

Melanie immediately captured Krista's lips and pulled her close. The kiss continued as they both sank deeper into the pleasure coursing through their bodies.

Krista had never been kissed so thoroughly and completely she thought as she hung onto Melanie with warmth spreading through her body. Her hands stroked up and down Melanie's back as the kiss completely consumed her.

"Mmm," Melanie groaned as she pulled away. "Let's go in here." She grabbed Krista's hand, led them into the living area and pulled her down onto the couch with her. Melanie leaned back and rested her head on the arm of the couch bringing Krista on top of her. She cupped the side of Krista's face and said, "All I want to do is to keep kissing you."

"That's perfect because I don't want you to stop." Krista leaned in and joined their lips together again.

8

Melanie ran her hand up and down Krista's back as her head rested on her chest. *I could get used to this,* she thought. "Did you think this was how your night would turn out when you walked up with that beer?"

"I was hopeful."

"Seriously?" Melanie said, raising Krista's chin with her finger.

"A girl can dream. You may have imagined kissing me, but I've imagined a few other things and this would be one." She grinned then kissed Melanie on the lips. "But I didn't know if you felt the same way."

"You didn't? Shit, Krissy, you had me the first day we met."

"The first day?"

"Yes. You were so good with the girls, and the way you looked into my eyes... You saw me. I wasn't just a single mom to you; you looked at me and saw a woman."

"A very beautiful woman. My heart was beating out of my chest. You do that to me all the time."

"I feel it, too."

Krista propped up on her elbows and stared into Melanie's eyes. She leaned down and kissed her tenderly. Melanie deepened the kiss as their tongues met and they both moaned. She pulled Krista closer and wrapped her leg around her. This woman made her body come alive like it hadn't in years. She had to slow down because she didn't want to scare Krista away, but it felt so good to want someone again.

Krista pulled back and they both were breathing hard.

"Can you spend the night?" asked Melanie. She could see the indecision on Krista's face and waited.

She closed her eyes and shook her head. "This is going to sound so lame. I still live with my parents."

"That's not lame. Of course you do. You're home from college for the summer."

"Out of respect to them I try not to stay out too late and let them know where I'm going to be so they won't worry."

"Do they know you're here?"

"Yes, but I didn't say I was staying the night. Besides, I have to work tomorrow for Julia."

"What about tomorrow night? Would you stay?"

A smile lit Krista's face. "Yes! I'd love to."

Melanie matched Krista's smile. *I'm thirty-three years old with a seven- and eight-year-old, but I'm not passing up this opportunity to be with this amazing woman*, she told herself. "Listen, you're welcome to stay any night you want, even if the girls are here. They'd love it and you know I would too. So let this be your invitation for the rest of the summer. Okay?"

"Are you sure?"

"Yes, I'm sure. We've both been tip-toeing around this since we got here. I don't want to waste a minute of time with you." Melanie couldn't believe she'd said that. "Oh no! I've scared you off!" she winced, closing her eyes.

She felt smiling lips on hers. As she returned the kiss, Krista's fingers trailed down her cheek until her hand rested on Melanie's chest. "You haven't scared me away," she whispered. "I want to be here with you."

"It's been a very long time since I've felt wanted or wanted anyone back, Kris. I'm a bit overwhelmed, but at the same time I know there is something special going on here."

Krista smiled. "I have felt drawn to you since our eyes met that very first day, too. I agree; let's not waste a minute."

Melanie sighed in relief. She'd felt the same thing and didn't want to spend the summer wondering when they could spend it playing, laughing, kissing, and more instead.

"Do you remember the surprise I mentioned earlier?" Krista asked.

"Yes. You said it had to be dark."

"It's dark enough," Krista said, wiggling her eyebrows. "Don't look so suspicious. You said you trusted me."

"I do," Melanie said.

"Come with me," she said, standing and offering Melanie her hand.

Melanie took it, letting Krista pull her up, and Krista led them outside down to the water.

"Let's go swimming," Krista said as they approached the sand.

"Okay, but I don't have my swimsuit on."

"You don't need it," said Krista, stepping out of her sandals. "Have you ever been skinny dipping?"

"No." Melanie grinned and looked around.

"No one will see us," Krista said, taking her shirt and then her shorts off.

Melanie couldn't keep from staring at Krista's toned and tan body.

"You're staring. You've seen me many times like this."

"I know, but I don't have to hide my feelings now. You are beautiful, Krista."

"Thank you, but come on," she said, taking her bra and panties off and walking into the water.

Melanie quickly got out of her clothes and followed Krista into the calm water.

"Oh my God, Krista. This feels incredible."

"Doesn't it? Come on, gorgeous," she said, offering Melanie her hand.

She walked them deeper until the water reached just above their breasts.

Krista was a couple inches shorter than Melanie so she put her arms around Melanie's shoulders and wrapped her legs around her middle, letting her support them.

"Isn't this nice?" Krista whispered in Melanie's ear. Then she nibbled her ear lobe and swirled her tongue inside her ear.

"Good God, Krista," Melanie moaned. She trailed her hands down Krista's back and cupped her ass cheeks, keeping her close.

"Mmm, if we weren't in water you'd feel how wet I am for you right this minute, Mel," she whispered.

"God," Melanie groaned, letting her head drop back. The desire to touch and taste Krista was almost too much. She slid her hands up Krista's sides and between them so she could cup Krista's breasts.

Krista moaned and kissed down from Melanie's ear to the pulse point on her neck. When Melanie pinched her nipples Krista said breathlessly, "Oh Mel, that feels so good." She gently bit her shoulder. "I won't leave a mark, but you're driving me wild." Then she grabbed Melanie's face and kissed her passionately.

As their heartbeats soared, their tongues danced and the water lapped gently around them. Melanie tore her lips away and panted, looking fiercely into Krista's eyes. "I don't want our first time to be rushed. I want to touch you and taste you and kiss you all night long."

Krista nodded, breathing heavily. "I can't wait until tomorrow night."

Melanie smiled and leaned back into the water. "I've got to cool off. Come on."

Krista grinned and they floated on their backs holding hands.

"Would you want to go on a boat ride with Julia and Heidi tomorrow?"

"I thought you were working for Julia tomorrow."

"I am. Heidi is her girlfriend. She's visiting for the weekend and wants to go out in the boat. I get off at 4:00 and we could go with them since you're a guest and I'm your favorite driver."

"Mmm, you're my favorite in a lot of things," she said, squeezing her hand. "Are you sure they'd want to hang out with me?"

"Why do you say it like that?" Krista asked, pulling Melanie into her arms.

"Have you noticed I'm a little older than you?"

"Have you noticed I'm younger than you?" Krista said, challenging her.

Melanie could see Krista's eyes sparkling in the moonlight and they were mesmerizing. "I don't notice it when we're together. It's when we're apart that I think about it."

"That's because you're thinking of bad things when you should be thinking about all the good things. Like this," Krista said, kissing her on the lips. "And this." She kissed her neck. "And this." She rubbed her hand over the cheeks of her ass, coming around to gently run her fingers through the coarse hairs between her legs.

"Mmm, those are all very good things to think about," Melanie said dreamily, bringing their lips together once again. How she'd missed the feel of a woman in her arms and on her lips, or was it this woman that made the difference?

"You know Julia and you'll like Heidi. She's in her final year of law school. You can talk about serious things with her."

"I can't talk about serious things with you?"

"Well, because I'm in the performing arts I'm not always taken seriously."

"That's poor judgement on whomever is doing that. I've seen the brain inside that incredibly beautiful head of yours. I have no doubt you'll change the world someday, Krista Kyle."

"Wow! I don't know about that."

"I do. We've had plenty of serious talks in our time together and I've heard the things you've shared with the girls about kindness and working hard. You don't think your piercing blue eyes and luxurious thick dark brown hair is what got my attention do you?"

"I don't know," Krista said, suddenly timid.

"Is that what you think of me?" Melanie continued to probe.

"Gosh no. Yes, you are extremely beautiful, but it's your heart that grabbed my attention. You make everyone feel important; like they matter. And that's what drew me to you. That's why in such a short time you matter so much to me."

Melanie smiled and ran her fingers along Krista's cheek. "You do matter. And just so you know, it's the way those blue eyes look at me. I can't wait to run my fingers through those thick beautiful brown locks of yours."

Krista smiled and looked down again.

"Don't be shy about compliments, darling. You take them, every one."

"I'm lucky to have good genes from my Mam-maw and I've heard about my beauty since I was young. But the way you say it and the way you look at me makes me feel beautiful."

"You are incredibly so and you're fun. I can't believe you've taken me skinny dipping."

"I can't believe you ran into the water so quickly and didn't let me get a look at you."

"Because I was chasing after you."

They began to walk back toward the beach arm in arm. Krista walked over to her clothes and began to put them on.

"We don't have to get dressed to walk back inside, do we?" Melanie said, emboldened in her nakedness.

"If I go back inside I won't leave. And it's too late to call my parents."

Melanie watched her slip into her shorts and put her shirt back on without her bra. "What am I supposed to do all day until you get off?"

Krista chuckled. "I'll try to come by around lunch. That's when we usually do the trash run for these cabins on Saturday. You can enjoy that peace and quiet you talked about earlier."

"You know I was teasing you."

"No I did not! I thought I'd really messed up."

"No you didn't or you wouldn't have come by in the first place."

"It doesn't matter now anyway. I like being straight forward and out in the open," Krista said, winking.

"In all seriousness, I do too," she said, taking Krista's hand. "I meant what I said. I don't want to waste any time we have together." She kissed Krista quickly and put her shirt and shorts back on.

They walked to Krista's car and she said, "Do I need to pick up anything in town for you?"

"Nope. All I need is for you to come back."

Krista put her arms around Melanie's neck and stared into her eyes. "Thank you for a wonderful evening."

"My pleasure," Melanie said, leaning in and kissing Krista softly. Her arms were on Krista's hips and she pulled her closer. The feel of this woman against her brought a rush of emotions to her heart. They stayed like that, simply holding one another for a few minutes.

"See you tomorrow, gorgeous," Krista said, kissing Melanie's cheek. She got in her car and lowered the window.

"Just one more," Melanie said, leaning in and kissing her. "I'll always need one more."

Krista smiled. "I'll always have one for you."

Melanie kissed her one more time and stepped back as she put the car in gear. She watched her back up and turn onto the road. She stayed there until Krista's red tail lights disappeared around the bend in the road.

She let out a deep breath. There were so many things that could go wrong with this, but for now she didn't care. Krista had awakened something inside her the first time their eyes locked and she didn't want to hide it anymore.

9

Could this day go any slower? Krista thought. She'd had to do everything she could not to go by Melanie's before work. Honestly, she was a bit afraid because she knew it would be even harder to leave. This made her smile to herself. A few kisses and she was wild about Melanie Zimmer.

She'd been busy helping in the restaurant and kitchen, restocking the bar, cleaning up around the beach, and making sure the bikes were available for the guests. Earlier that morning, she had gotten two of the boats ready for morning rentals and put away all the floats, life jackets, and various water toys that appeared on the dock.

She looked at her watch and grinned. It was finally time to do the trash run for the cabins and more importantly see Melanie. Her heart skipped a beat just thinking about her. She wondered if this is what it felt like to be in love. There were a couple of girls she'd dated in college and liked very much, but this had felt different from the very start.

"Mr. Bailey, I'm taking the pickup to do the trash run at the cabins," she called to the owner and her boss.

"Thanks Krista," he said. "The big plastic trash cans are down at the beach. I needed them this morning."

"Okay, see you later."

She hopped in the pickup and stopped by the beach to throw the big cans in the back. Then she sped off to get her job done. Her last stop would be Melanie's and she absolutely couldn't wait to see her.

She made quick work of the other cabins and pulled into Melanie's place. She walked around to the back and found her lying on the chaise lounge reading a book. When Melanie saw her, the biggest smile grew on her face.

Krista leaned down and put her hands on the arms of the lounge chair. She paused for a moment and said, "I need this." Then she touched her lips to Melanie's and the world fell away. She felt Melanie's hands slide around her back as she pulled her down on top of her.

"Mmm," Melanie moaned. "I needed that, too." She looked into Krista's eyes and said, "And this." She claimed Krista's lips with a hot, wet passionate kiss that they both had been longing for.

After a few moments they pulled apart and grinned at one another.

"Now I feel like I can breathe again," Melanie admitted.

"I know," Krista said cupping the side of her face. "It's been the longest morning. I wanted to come by so bad!"

"Why didn't you?" Melanie said, turning her head and kissing the palm of Krista's hand.

"Because I knew I wouldn't leave. I'm weak, you've done something to me," she said honestly. "And I like it," she added, bringing their lips together for another searing kiss. "I'll come here as soon as I get off and we can meet Julia and Heidi at the dock. Is that okay?"

"I'll be waiting," Melanie said softly, running her fingers through Krista's hair. "You've done something to me too, Krista Kyle. You've put me under your spell."

Krista kissed Melanie again. It began tender and soft and sweet, but then she couldn't stop the heat building inside her. She knew Melanie felt it too because her arms tightened, melding them chest to chest. *I can't wait to do this tonight with nothing between us, just skin on skin*, Krista thought.

Finally she pulled back and whispered, "I have to go."

Melanie closed her eyes. "Okay, but let me up. Don't leave yet."

Krista got up and Melanie ran into the cabin. She came out just as quickly with a paper sack.

"I made you a pimento cheese sandwich. I was afraid you wouldn't have time for lunch."

Krista took the bag with the most amazed look on her face.

"Oh no. You don't like pimento cheese. I can make something else. It'll only take a minute."

"No," Krista said, wrapping her arms around Melanie and hugging her.

"Okay? You like pimento cheese?" she said, hugging her back.

Krista let her go and said, "My first job was as a lifeguard at the municipal pool. My mom would bring me a pimento cheese sandwich every day for lunch. This is so incredibly sweet, Mel."

"Just so you know, I wasn't having motherly thoughts when I made it," Melanie said, giving Krista a devilish grin.

Krista chuckled and shook her head. Melanie Zimmer had just stolen her heart and she couldn't wait to see what she did with it.

"What's going on in that head of yours, Krissy?" she asked, putting her hand on the back of Krista's neck and pulling her in for a kiss.

"You take my breath away, Mel," Krista whispered, her eyes closed and forehead resting on Melanie's.

"I know. Don't be scared. It's okay; we'll be okay."

Krista opened her eyes and looked into the softest, most beautiful brown eyes. She didn't feel afraid; she felt safe and excited. "I'm not scared. I've never felt this before, Mel. Can we talk more about it tonight?"

"Of course we can. But a very wise woman told me to only think of the good things," she said, smiling and cupping the side of Krista's face.

"A wise woman, huh. There's only good things when I think about you." Krista leaned in and kissed her one more time.

Melanie slid her hand into Krista's and walked her to the pickup. "You'll be here around 4:00?"

"Yeah," Krista said, kissing the back of Melanie's hand. "Thanks for the sandwich."

"You're welcome," Melanie said as Krista climbed into the pickup. "I need one more if you expect me to make it through this afternoon," Melanie added, her eyes twinkling as her hands rested on the window sill. She looked around and leaned into the cab of the pickup, searching for Krista's lips.

Krista met her lips with her own and held them together with her hand on the back of Melanie's head, deepening the kiss. She sat back and sighed. "Dang! I could do that all day!"

Melanie laughed. "Hurry up so you can get back!"

Krista backed out with the biggest smile on her face. Thankfully the rest of the afternoon passed quickly. She was down at the dock getting the boat ready when Julia and Heidi walked up.

"Hey Superstar," Julia said, grinning.

"Hey yourself," she said, getting out of the boat. "Hi Heidi," she said, giving her a hug.

"Where's my hug?"

"I see you every day," Krista said, giving her a big hug and squeezing her tight.

"I bet you'll be hugging Melanie every day now, won't you?"

"Now what makes you say that?"

"Krista Kyle, I don't know what you did last night, but the happiness is shining on your face," teased Julia. "And I know it's because of Melanie Zimmer."

"Are you sure it's because of Melanie and not because I'm here?" Heidi asked playfully.

"I'm sure. You didn't call me last night or this morning," said Julia.

Krista shrugged. "I got home late and I knew you had your own plans."

"You didn't spend the night?" Julia teased.

"I am tonight," Krista said seductively.

"Tell me!" Julia squealed.

Krista chuckled. "Y'all, she's incredible," she continued dreamily.

"I already know that. Details, Krissy!"

"You'll see for yourself. She's coming with us!"

"Really!" said Heidi. "I can't wait to meet her."

"She wondered why we'd want to hang out with someone so old." Krista laughed.

"Old? She's not old."

"That's what I told her."

"Go get her. I'll finish this up."

"Okay." Krista grinned and hurried up the walkway.

"Krista, wait!" Julia yelled. "You've got all night so hurry back."

Krista laughed and waved then jumped in her car and sped off to Melanie's. She hopped out of her car with her bag and walked to the back of the cabin. She found Melanie sitting in one of the chairs at the beach.

Melanie turned around and grinned. "There she is."

"Hey there gorgeous."

"I can't tell you how good you look walking up to me with that bag in your hand."

"What?" Krista said, confused.

"It means you're staying and that makes me very happy," she said, wrapping her arms around Krista and holding her close. She pulled back and kissed her softly. "Let's go inside so you can change."

They walked to the cabin holding hands.

"I really like holding your hand. It's quickly become one of my favorite things," said Krista.

Melanie kissed the back of her hand and opened the back door.

Krista started taking her clothes off and Melanie said, "You can go in the bedroom."

"You don't want to see me naked?" she said, slipping her shorts off.

"I'm not looking because I know what will happen if I do," Melanie said, walking into the kitchen.

"Maybe we don't have to go in the boat after all," Krista said, getting her swimsuit out of her bag.

"No, I want to," Melanie said from the kitchen. She turned around as Krista pulled her bikini bottoms up. "But damn, honey. I don't see us getting much sleep tonight."

Krista giggled and took her bra off, replacing it with her bikini top. She watched Melanie watch her and normally it would make her self-conscious, but not the way Melanie looked at her. Krista knew she wanted her, but Mel looked at her with desire and respect and wonder.

"Fuck," she breathed out.

Melanie cocked her head. "What?"

"The way you look at me, Mel. It makes me feel…" Krista said, not finishing.

Melanie walked over and took her hands. "Adored? Worshipped? Cared for?"

Krista nodded.

Melanie kissed her softly. "We'll talk more tonight. Okay?"

"Okay." Krista smiled and kissed her back.

"I have beer to take with us and a few snacks," she said, walking to the kitchen and picking up a bag. She handed a six pack of beer to Krista and winked. "I want to go today because I want to meet your friends. Well, I know Julia. But also out on the lake we don't have to worry about anyone seeing us. I can hold your hand or put my arm around you or kiss you without worrying about someone staring or someone here finding out. I'm pretty sure the Baileys would frown on it."

"They would," she said, walking to the door. "Don't worry about that now, let's go have some fun."

Melanie kissed her quickly as they walked into the backyard and to Krista's car.

10

Julia and Heidi were waiting for Krista and Melanie in the boat. After quick introductions they were whizzing across the lake, the wind in their hair and sunshine on their faces. Krista reached out her hand to Melanie and steered the boat with the other. After a quick squeeze she looked behind her to see Julia and Heidi sitting side by side. Julia had her arm around Heidi and was yelling something in her ear over the noise of the motor combined with the wind.

What a wonderful day, Krista thought as she looked over at Melanie and grinned. As if reading her thoughts Melanie leaned over and kissed her cheek and yelled in her ear. "You look stunning!"

Krista gave her a confused look along with a grin.

Melanie shouted, "Your face is full of happiness, your eyes are bright, and you're glowing."

Krista nodded. "You know why!" she shouted.

"Do I?" Melanie mouthed with her eyebrows raised.

Krista looked around to be sure there weren't any boats in their path and then grabbed Melanie around the back of her neck. She pulled her in for a quick kiss. "That's why!" she shouted.

Julia and Heidi whooped from the back of the boat and Melanie's face matched Krista's with happiness.

They sped along, enjoying the freedom of skimming over the water and the promise of good times to come. Krista nudged the throttle back and the boat started to slow down.

"Let's jump off the cliffs," she said to the group.

"What?" Heidi asked, her voice uncertain.

"Look." Krista pointed. Just ahead, a small mountain of rocks rose from the water. They formed a set of cliffs that were different heights above the water. There were a few boats anchored in front of the cliff face and people were in various stages of climbing up the rocks or jumping off. Whoops of delight, along with laughter and splashing water reached their ears as Krista turned the motor off.

"It's fun!" said Julia, standing up. "I'll hold your hand."

Heidi stayed seated, watching the jumpers with indecision clouding her face.

"I was scared my first time too, Heidi," said Melanie. "Krista brought me and the girls over the second day we were here. They swam over, climbed up like it wasn't anything." She looked over at Krista and smirked. "My youngest was waving at me and jumped off. She came up laughing and said, 'Come on Mommy, I'll hold your hand.' I had to jump then."

Krista laughed. "And you loved it, didn't you?"

"I did," she said, grinning at Krista.

"Well, I don't know that I can trust these two," Heidi said, indicating Julia and Krista. "But you, I trust."

"Oh so that's how you're going to be," said Julia playfully. "Then let Melanie hold your hand."

"Nope," Krista said firmly. "Melanie is holding my hand."

"Okay then. Come on cutie, I'll hold your hand," Julia said, reaching her hand to Heidi.

They threw the anchor out and all jumped in the water. They took turns jumping off the cliffs and Krista even got Melanie to try one of the taller bluffs. After they got back in the boat, Krista drove them around to the other side of the point the cliffs made in the water. Over there, the mountain gently sloped upward and the water was calm.

Once again they threw out the anchor and each took a life jacket and jumped in the water. They put their feet in the life jackets' arms and wore them like a diaper. The jacket kept them afloat but didn't restrict their movements.

Before jumping in Krista put a tape in the boom box and turned it up. "How's that? Can you hear it?"

"That's good," answered Julia.

"This is the life," Heidi said, leaning her head back into the water.

"Yeah it is," said Julia. Just then a song came on from Carol King's *Tapestry*. "Sing for us, Krista!"

"Oh no, not now," Krista said.

"Has she told you that you're going to get the chance to see her perform, Melanie?"

"No she hasn't," Melanie said, staring at Krista.

"I figured. Next month her theater group is coming to the lake," said Julia.

"And?" Melanie said to Krista.

"We have a group that performs short one act skits and a few musical numbers," explained Krista. "They'll put up a little stage in the lawn area between the beach and the restaurant."

"When do you rehearse? Are you leaving?" asked Melanie.

"No. These are skits we did for a spring class. The group will get here Friday night. We'll rehearse on Saturday and then perform Saturday night. Our local high school drama teacher does a drama camp for elementary, junior high and high school kids during the summer. They get the chance to work with us and our professors. The teacher has known my professor for years and they do this every summer."

"You'll get to see why I call her Superstar. She not only sings like an angel, but she can act!"

"Stop, Jules!" Krista said, her eyes wide.

"I have to agree, Krista. I got to see her sing and act for the first time in their spring performance back in April. She was incredible," Heidi said to Melanie.

Krista hid her face on Melanie's shoulder. "I'm not surprised and I can't wait. The girls will love it," Melanie said. "When is it?" She tilted Krista's face up.

"Saturday, the sixteenth," Krista said, looking up into Melanie's eyes.

"Oh no! They stay with their dad for two weeks in July and that's right in the middle of it," Melanie said sadly. "I guess that means I get the star of the show all to myself?" she asked, putting her arms around Krista's neck.

"You'll be able to impress all your friends when you tell them you knew Krista Kyle when she was becoming a star. Hollywood watch out!" Julia said.

"Are you going to Hollywood?" Melanie asked excitedly.

"That's the plan. After I graduate next May my professor has auditions set up for a few of us in June."

Melanie gasped. "How exciting!"

"I still have to get through this year and I have a lot left to learn."

"But still, Krista. That's incredible."

"I hope so. When I become rich and famous will you invest my money for me?" asked Krista.

"I sure will. No charge," said Melanie.

"Oh I think I know a few ways I can pay you," Krista said, kissing her.

"Wait? You do investments?" asked Heidi.

"I do. I'm a financial planner. When I divorced six years ago I took my half of our settlement and invested in a couple of businesses that have since taken off. That's how I can be here all summer. When I get back I'm starting my own investment firm."

"Wow! Then Julia's the one you'll want. She's a business major and so much smarter than any of us.'"

Julia chuckled. "Well, thanks honey, but I'm not sure I'll be looking for a job around Houston."

"And why is that, Jules? Do you want to stay in Dallas near a certain gay lawyer we all know and love?" Krista teased.

"Maybe," she said, not giving anything away.

"Does everyone know you're gay, Heidi?" asked Melanie. "Oops, that was too personal. You don't have to answer that."

"No, it's okay. Yes, my family does know. I was lucky to grow up with an accepting family. I have an uncle who is gay and that helped my parents to see that I wasn't doomed like so many people believe. But I don't broadcast it at school and probably won't in my first job until I can see how accepting the firm I work for is. However, I volunteer at a Gay and Lesbian Alliance. We're working on equal rights."

"Wow, that's brave."

"It helps that I grew up in a large city and there were other gay people in my school, unlike here for Julia and Krista."

"Yeah, my parents don't know," said Julia. "I'll tell them some day."

"My professor told us that in Hollywood there's a group of gay and lesbians actors and actresses that everyone knows about, but the reporters don't write about them. He said it's common knowledge, but it's not talked about. They have these lavish parties that get wild."

"You don't plan on telling anyone when you get there?" asked Melanie.

"No. I don't think it would be safe for my career. Maybe if I'm lucky and get a role on a TV show or commercials then eventually I could, but not until I'm sure."

"I'm not sure how I would explain it to my kids. It's much better than it was when I was in college. Do you think your small town would accept you?" Melanie asked Krista and Julia.

"I don't know. We do live in rural Texas and I wouldn't say that's gay friendly," said Julia.

"I'm sure it will get better. We have to be brave like the women that came before us."

"I agree, but I'm not ready to be brave here, not just yet," said Krista. "Maybe in a city like where you live, Mel, it would be different." Melanie nodded.

"We don't have to worry about that out here though," said Julia. "I think it's time for a beer."

"It's your turn to get them," Krista said.

Julia swam over to the boat and threw each one of them a beer then she stopped the tape and turned the radio on. "Krista! Listen!"

"Turn it up!" Krista yelled and started singing along with Tears For Fears's song, "Shout." Everyone joined as they sang at the top of their voices and then laughed.

Krista swam over to Melanie and put her arms around her neck and stared into her eyes. She called over to Julia, but never looked away, "Anyplace else y'all want to go, Jules?" A small smile adorned Melanie's face as she read the look in Krista's eyes.

"Nope. Are you ready to go back?" Julia asked.

"Yep." Krista slowly smiled at Melanie and then gently kissed her lips.

"Okay. I'll drive back," Julia said, swimming to the boat.

"Are you ready?" Krista asked Melanie quietly.

"So ready," she answered softly.

They joined Heidi and Julia on the boat, pulled up anchor and took their seats in the back. Melanie slipped her arm around Krista and pulled her into her side. *This feels perfect*, Krista thought as she closed her eyes and sank a little deeper into Melanie.

11

"We're going up to the restaurant for dinner. Do y'all want to join us?" Julia asked as they got out of the boat.

Krista looked over at Melanie with a 'please say no' expression on her face.

"I made a little something for us at the cabin," she said with a gaze toward Krista. "Would y'all like to come with us?" she asked politely.

Julia smiled at Krista and then looked at Melanie. "No thanks, but that's nice of you to ask. This was fun today."

"Yeah it was," agreed Heidi.

"Y'all go ahead, we'll clean up everything here," said Julia.

"No. We'll help," said Melanie.

"No you won't!" said Julia. "Krista worked for me today so I could spend time with Heidi. Go enjoy your evening."

"Thanks Jules. See y'all tomorrow," Krista said, quickly grabbing Melanie's hand and pulling her toward the walkway.

"Bye!" Melanie yelled over her shoulder.

Krista dropped her hand before anyone could see them and hurried to the car. She drove them to Melanie's cabin and when they got out she said, "That was fun today."

"Yeah, it was," Melanie said, taking her hand as they walked around to the back door.

"Did you really make something for dinner?" asked Krista.

Melanie pulled Krista into the kitchen and then into her arms and kissed her. It quickly became heated and Melanie pulled away. "As much as I'd like to get you naked," she said, breathing hard, "you're more than just sex to me."

"I know that."

"Do you? Have a seat and I'll feed you," Melanie said, nodding toward the kitchen table.

"I can help," Krista said.

"Let me do this, please."

Krista smiled and sat down as Melanie started getting things out of the refrigerator. "It's not much. I made a salad and have fruit," she said, setting the fruit on the table. "Do you like strawberries?"

"I do."

Melanie put the salad in bowls and set them on the table. She sat down next to Krista and took a strawberry between her fingers. "Try this," she said, holding it to Krista's mouth.

She slowly took the strawberry into her mouth, her eyes never leaving Melanie's. "Mmm," she murmured. "Sweet." She swallowed. "Mel, I've never felt like this before," she said, suddenly overcome with emotion.

Melanie didn't say anything, waiting for Krista to continue.

"I've never been in love. I've dated and thought I might be a couple of times. Julia told me I'd know when it happened. That's the way it was for her with Heidi. She said kisses are sweeter and sex is even better. I can't believe I feel comfortable enough to tell you this; that's how I know this is different."

Melanie smiled at Krista with such affection. "I didn't think I'd ever feel like this again for anyone. I won't say it's love at first sight, Krista. But I do believe our hearts connected and have been bringing us ever closer since we met."

"That's why I can't stay away from you."

"Have you noticed how many times the girls and I have looked for you? This isn't one night just because the girls aren't here. You know that, right?"

Krista nodded.

She cupped Krista's face and kissed her gently. "Let me show you how I feel." Melanie got up and took Krista's hand and led them to the bedroom.

She stopped at the foot of the bed and turned to Krista. Her eyes met Krista's and then she reached for the bottom of her shirt and pulled it over her head. Melanie took one finger and began at Krista's cheek and trailed it down her neck and over her collarbone. Then she slowly guided it between her breasts and stopped at the band to her bikini top. Her gaze followed where her finger had been until it met Krista's eyes.

Krista was on fire! Her chest was moving up and down as Melanie's eyes burned into hers. Those brown eyes were dark and she melted into them. This had to be love, she thought, because nothing could feel better than the way Melanie was looking at her. Sure, she could see desire, but she also saw love. Melanie loved her and was about to show her.

Just when Krista didn't think she could wait any longer, Melanie reached up behind her neck and untied the top to her bikini. Then she reached around and unhooked the back, tossing it to the floor.

"You are so beautiful, Kris," Melanie whispered against Krista's lips and then kissed her softly.

Krista felt her heart stop and her legs weakened, but Melanie's strong hands were on her shoulders, turning her towards the bed. She felt the back of her knees touch the bed and Melanie gently pushed her down. Then she reached for her shorts and quickly slid those off her legs along with her bikini bottoms.

"Wait," Krista said.

"It's okay." Melanie gave her a smile as she quickly removed her shirt and swimsuit top. Then she walked between Krista's legs and put her hands on her shoulders.

Krista looked up at her with a smile and hooked her thumbs into the sides of Melanie's shorts, pulling them and her swim bottoms off at the same time. Then she pulled Melanie to her and wrapped her arms around her middle, resting her head against her chest. She could hear Melanie's heart beating and feel her fingers running through her hair. She eased her head back and looked up at her. "Kiss me," she whispered.

Melanie bent down and captured Krista's lips in a scorching kiss. When their tongues met Krista gasped. She laid back and eased up the bed, pulling Mel on top of her. This is what she'd been waiting on. She wanted to feel Melanie's skin on hers. And then Melanie's thigh was between her legs and she spread them wider.

Melanie began to trail kisses from Krista's ear down her neck and along her shoulder. She kissed back across Krista's collarbone and then trailed her tongue down between her breasts and across, swirling it around her nipple.

"Oh Mel," Krista exhaled.

"Mmm," Melanie murmured as she swirled round and round and then touched the tip of her now hard nipple.

Krista moaned again and Melanie sucked her nipple into her mouth. She playfully bit down and then sucked as Krista's hands combed through Melanie's hair.

"Melanie," she whispered.

Melanie moaned and kissed her way across to Krista's other breast, giving it her attention.

"That feels so good," Krista moaned. She could feel Melanie smile as she bit down on her nipple once again.

"You're incredible, Kris," Melanie said the words between kisses as she settled between Krista's legs.

She ran her hands up Krista's thighs and around to the back of her legs. Krista bent her knees and Melanie kissed from there down the inside of each thigh to where they met.

"God Mel," Krista groaned, letting her legs fall open.

"Krista," Melanie whispered and then ran her tongue along the length of Krista's center.

"Oh yes," groaned Krista. Her hips bucked and Melanie splayed her hands over Krista's thighs, holding her in place.

Melanie licked up and down and around Krista's throbbing clit. She looked up and saw Krista looking down at her. "Your taste is the honey I didn't realize I've longed for," she said. "I have to have you, Kris."

Then she sucked that pulsating bundle in and groaned as if feasting on the best thing she'd ever had in her mouth. Krista's head fell back on the pillow and one hand fisted the blanket as the other grabbed Melanie's hair and held on.

"Fuck, Mel," she said loudly. "Yes!"

Melanie's tongue began to flick across Krista's most sensitive spot as her finger teased Krista's opening.

"Mmm," Krista moaned over and over.

Melanie pushed one finger inside and exclaimed breathlessly, "Oh Krista!" Then she added another finger and began a slow rhythm. Krista rocked right along with her as they both moaned with pleasure.

"Kiss me, Mel," Krista said, raising her head and reaching for her lover.

Melanie gave her one more lick and continued her rhythm as she found Krista's mouth. Krista wrapped her arms around Melanie and kissed her with passion. She moaned and groaned through the kisses as she came closer and closer. It all felt so good. Melanie was inside, but Krista was wrapped around her. Their kisses were hot and wet and then Krista pulled her mouth away to look into Melanie's eyes.

Right then Melanie curled her fingers and found that perfect place inside her. Krista said, "I love you, Mel." And then she exploded inside. She felt a wave of warmth and happiness fly through her body up and down and back again. Her eyes closed and she held onto Melanie until finally she couldn't any longer. She fell back panting and her heart was full of love that Melanie put there.

"My God, Mel," she said, opening her eyes. The moment was almost too much as she felt tears prickle there. Then she could see those soft velvety brown eyes swimming in love for her. She was sure Melanie felt it too.

"I love you, too, Krista," she whispered, burying her head in Krista's neck.

Krista stroked her naked back with one hand and cradled the back of her head with the other. "Hey," she said. "Are you okay?"

Melanie looked up with the biggest smile on her face. "I'm so much better than okay," she said, kissing Krista long and slow. She propped up on her elbow and looked down at Krista's blissed out expression.

"I didn't think anything could feel better than the way you look at me, but wow am I wrong," said Krista, grinning.

"Oh yeah?" Melanie played.

"You know exactly what I mean. You just filled my heart with love, Mel."

"I wanted to show you how I feel. I always want you to feel loved and adored."

"Oh baby I do," said Krista, cupping Melanie's cheek with her hand. She raised up and pushed Melanie on her back. For a moment she stared down at that beautiful woman and couldn't quite believe Melanie loved her, but she did and it was the best feeling in the world, she thought, smiling.

"What?" asked Melanie, smoothing Krista's hair back.

"My body has so much to tell your body. Words just won't do. And it starts with this," Krista said, bringing her lips softly down on Melanie's.

12

Melanie felt heavy, weighed down, when she began to awaken. Before opening her eyes she smiled because she realized Krista was wrapped around her. She had one leg slung over hers and one arm tightly around her middle with her head resting on Melanie's shoulder. She could feel as well as hear her slumbered breathing. Was there any better way to wake up? They hadn't slept much; just when she thought she couldn't keep her eyes open Krista would kiss her and wake up the desire inside her all over again.

This woman made her feel things she'd only ever imagined or read about in romance novels. She couldn't get enough of her. Krista could look at her and make her heart begin to thump. In a few short weeks Melanie had learned that Krista was kind and thoughtful; she was smart and had a plan for her life; but she was also fun and exciting and they'd been falling in love right alongside her girls since the day they'd met.

But two days ago they couldn't have stopped that first kiss, though neither of them tried. She didn't know if she believed in fate or karma or whatever, but they were going down this path together, right now, and that's what mattered. They had a whole summer to fill with love, laughter, and one another, then they'd figure out the rest. Melanie took in a satisfied breath and let it out.

"Mmm." Krista stirred. She kissed Melanie's chest and mumbled, "Good morning, lover."

Melanie giggled.

"I've always wanted to say that," Krista said, raising her head. She pecked Melanie on the cheek and smiled.

"I've just found the best way to wake up is with you in my arms."

"Hmm, I don't think so," Krista said, tilting her head and raising up over Melanie. "This is better," she said, pressing her lips to Melanie's firmly. She deepened the kiss and Melanie felt her heart speed up as well as her breathing.

"How do you do that?" she asked breathlessly when Krista pulled away. "One kiss and you make me melt."

"You're going to do more than melt," Krista said, beginning a slow quest down Melanie's body, leaving kisses in her wake. "You are so beautiful and I have to kiss you," Krista said, swirling her tongue around one nipple and then the other. She kissed over Melanie's stomach and down to the inside of each thigh.

Melanie had her hands in Krista's hair, but when she began nibbling on her inner thighs she arched her back and dug her hands into the bedsheets. "Oh Krista, my Krista," Melanie moaned, her head digging into the pillow. This woman lit such a fire inside her, Melanie thought. She had never wanted anyone the way she wanted Krista and right now Krista was everywhere. Her tongue was sliding through Melanie's wet folds, up and down and then around. Krista had reached a hand up to cup Melanie's breast and gave her nipple a pinch.

"Shit, Kris! That feels good." Melanie writhed beneath her.

"Mm, you taste so good," Krista said and then sucked Melanie's throbbing clit into her mouth as she pinched her nipple again.

"Oh God!"

But Krista wasn't done. She took her other hand and gently pushed two fingers inside, causing another loud grateful moan from Melanie.

"Krista," she murmured over and over as pleasure radiated through her body. "Yes," she breathed as Krista started a rhythm that her hips matched. It wasn't long until the orgasm began to build and her body began to quiver. When release came every muscle in her body flexed. She could feel the love that Krista was wrapping her in and it was unbelievable, undeniable, and felt better than anything she'd ever experienced. Her body finally let go and she fell back on the bed in a heap.

Krista propped on her elbow and gazed at Melanie's pleased face as she caught her breath. She gave her a wry smile and said, "Now, isn't that a better way to wake up?"

Melanie grinned at her then grabbed her face and kissed her hard, their lips smacking. "Yes, it is." She paused, then added, "Lover."

Krista's face lit up with delight.

"Hey," Melanie said, toying with the ends of Krista's hair. "Why don't you go with me to pick up the girls today? They would love it and I think you know how I'd feel about it." She grinned.

"Really?"

"Yes, it would be fun," Melanie said assuredly.

"Hmm," Krista mused. "When and where are you supposed to pick them up?"

"I'm meeting them at a park near their grandparents house at 5:00. It's close to SMU. Why?"

"I'd like to take you somewhere before we get them; it's on the way. Do you trust me?"

Melanie grinned. "You've asked me that before and my answer is still yes."

Krista returned her grin and kissed her excitedly.

"But we don't have to leave for a while," Melanie said, rolling over on top of Krista. She paused before kissing her and said seriously, "I love you, Krista."

"I know," Krista whispered, her breath already ragged. "Show me."

* * *

"Turn here," Krista said, directing Melanie into a parking lot. "This is it," she said excitedly.

Melanie looked at a one story building with no windows and a double door at the front. Over the door was a simple sign that said *Jugs*. "Is this what I think it is?" she asked, looking over at Krista.

"If you think it's a lesbian bar then you're right."

"Jugs? Really?"

Krista laughed. "Yep. It's not busy on a Sunday afternoon and I thought we could sip a beer and dance. I really want to dance with you."

"You do?" Melanie asked, her face softening with emotion.

Krista nodded. "Come on," she said, getting out of the car.

They walked in and Krista immediately grabbed her hand. There were two women at the bar and two others sitting at a table off to the side. Krista ordered two beers and led Melanie to a table by the dance floor.

"Do you come here a lot?" Melanie asked.

"Not really. I've been here a few times, mainly on Saturday nights when it gets crowded and loud."

"Did you come here with your girlfriend?"

"I did a couple of times and with Julia and Heidi." Krista took a sip of her beer and smiled at Melanie. "Do you want to be my girlfriend?"

Melanie grinned. "I thought I was your lover."

Krista shook her head and giggled. "You are." Then seriously she added, "And much more." She took Melanie's hand and continued. "I know now that the girls are back we won't have as much alone time, but I hope it doesn't change anything."

"The girls love you and I do too."

"You do realize that I've seen y'all every day since you first got here," said Krista.

"Did you not notice that if for whatever reason we hadn't seen you that me or the girls found you before you were finished for the day? I think our hearts knew before our heads caught up."

"I still want to spend time with y'all."

"I want that too. I'm just not ready for the girls to know that we're more than friends. I mean, your parents don't even know about you."

Krista nodded sadly. "I know. I hate that we have to hide it. It could affect us professionally, as well as personally. But you know what, we'll figure it out. There's no reason we can't be together the rest of the summer. No more sad talk. I want to dance with my lover," she said, winking. Krista got up and went to talk to the bartender and when she came back, music began to fill the bar.

"Will you dance with me?"

"I'd love to," Melanie said, taking Krista's hand.

Krista took Melanie's hands and planted them on her hips and then put her own hands on Melanie's shoulders. "I asked the bartender to play us a few slow songs so I could dance with my girlfriend."

Melanie beamed a smile that was only for Krista.

"Hold me tight," Krista said, pulling Melanie to her. "I want to burn this into the memory part of our brains so when we can't be together we can still feel our arms around one another."

Melanie looked into Krista's eyes and pulled her closer. "I can feel your heart beating next to mine."

"Me too," Krista said and gently placed her lips on Melanie's. "Remember this, babe."

Melanie closed her eyes and buried her face in Krista's hair. They swayed and slowly circled to the music.

"Did you ever dance with your friend in college?" Krista asked, looking into Melanie's eyes.

"No. This is a first. It's the first time I've been in a gay bar."

"You are becoming so many firsts for me too, Mel," said Krista.

Melanie leaned in and kissed Krista tenderly. The song ended and the beat picked up. Krista grinned, put her arms in the air and began to move. Melanie followed her lead and they danced with abandon.

"I knew it," Krista yelled.

"Knew what?"

"I knew you'd be a great dancer."

Melanie shook her head and laughed and continued to dance.

They stayed there another hour, dancing and holding one another close, making more memories before they had to leave to meet the girls.

Later, they pulled into the designated area of the park and saw the girls playing with their cousin as their grandparents looked on. Melanie had told her that she'd always gotten along with her ex-husband's parents so there wouldn't be any drama. She wasn't prepared, however, for the greeting the girls gave her when she got out of the car.

"Krista!" Stephanie yelled.

When Jennifer heard her sister she squealed, "Krista!"

"I told you," Melanie said, grinning at her.

The girls ran up and each one hugged her.

"Hey!" Melanie said, holding her arms out.

"Sorry, Mom," Stephanie said, laughing and giving her a hug. Jennifer followed her sister.

"Hi Sherry, hi Ted," Melanie said. "This is Krista, our new friend," she said, introducing her to the girls' grandparents.

"Oh we know all about Krista," Sherry said with a smile. "It's nice to meet you."

"Nice to meet you too," Krista said, smiling.

"Our granddaughters seem to be enjoying your establishment," said Ted with a friendly smile.

"Well, I have to say it was quiet over the weekend without them," Krista said, winking at the girls.

"Girls, introduce Krista to your cousin," Melanie said, smiling at Krista.

"Krista," said Stephanie. "This is Maggie."

"Hi Maggie. It's nice to meet you."

"Hi," Maggie said shyly.

"We had better get going," said Melanie. "I'm sure the girls were good while they were with you," she said to Sherry, looking at her daughters.

"They were angels," said Sherry.

"I'm not sure I believe that." Melanie grinned.

The girls got their bags and put them in the trunk and then hugged their grandparents and Maggie.

"It was nice to meet you," said Krista, getting in the car.

Melanie got in and turned to look at Krista and then the girls. She didn't think her heart had ever been this full. "I missed y'all," she said to the girls.

Krista turned to face the girls and said, "I missed you, too!"

The girls laughed and Krista looked at Melanie and winked. "Take us home, Mom."

13

Krista, Melanie, and the girls fell into a pleasant rhythm as June turned into July. Krista had lunch with them nearly every day and went by after work. On weekends when Krista wasn't working they biked, swam, played games, or simply watched TV together.

At night when the girls went to bed Krista and Melanie were able to sneak kisses and hold one another close. Krista began to think this was what it would be like to have her own family and realized she was part of this one already and she liked it.

Julia would join them for lunch sometimes and also joined them on weekends occasionally. One day she had to go in and pick up supplies for the resort and asked the girls to go with her. This gave Krista and Melanie the opportunity to have lunch alone with no interruptions or need to be discreet.

They were naked, arms wrapped around one another still breathing hard when Krista said, "I'd better get dressed."

"The girls won't be back for a while."

"I know, but I am supposedly at work," Krista said, sitting up, but then she turned to look at Melanie. She was lying there, her brown hair fanned out across the pillow. She had one arm above her head and the other rested on Krista's back. "You are breathtaking," she said around the lump that had suddenly formed in her throat.

Instead of getting up she swung her leg around and straddled Melanie. She intertwined the fingers on both their hands and looked down at her with such love. "I'd marry you if I could."

Melanie's eyes widened and her eyebrows shot up her forehead.

"I could happily spend the rest of my life with you and the girls," Krista declared.

Melanie smiled. "But what about your career?"

"There are lots of things I can do with my career. Just know I love you that much, Melanie, and I can see our life together. Have you thought about it?"

"Of course I have, Kris. But there are so many things that go with it."

"I know. I think what I want you to know and to think about is that this isn't just for the summer anymore. I know it started that way, but Mel, I can't imagine my life without you in it. Okay?"

"Okay. I understand you want me to know how you feel and believe me I feel the same way. But next week we will take the girls to their dad for two weeks. Can we talk about it then? Because right now, with you on top of me like this, I really need you to kiss me before Julia brings them back. I need to feel you, Kris," she said with a hint of desperation in her voice and love in her eyes.

"God I love you," Krista said, crashing her lips on Melanie's.

"I love you, too," Melanie said between kisses. "I love your body on mine," she breathed.

Krista raised up quickly. "Can I spend the night?"

"What?" Melanie said.

Krista grinned and leaned down and kissed Melanie again. "I have an idea. May I spend the night with you?"

"You can spend every night with me from now on," Melanie said, spreading her arms out wide. "What's the idea?"

"Do you–" Krista started but Melanie interrupted her.

"Yes, I trust you," Melanie giggled.

"Wait until the girls get back," Krista said, grinning. "Now where were we? Oh yeah, I remember." Krista brought their lips together again for a fiery kiss.

A little later they had just finished putting their clothes back on and were holding one another, swaying to the music in their heads, when Krista heard Julia drive up in the truck.

"Do you promise to hold me all night long?" Krista asked sweetly.

"I do," Melanie said as they heard the truck doors close. They shared a quick kiss and then walked into the living area just as Julia came in the back door.

"We're back," she yelled a little too loudly.

Krista laughed. "We heard you."

Julia laughed along with her. "Just making sure," she said under her breath.

"Were you good helpers?" Melanie asked the girls.

"We were and look what Julia got us," Jennifer said, holding up a box of candy.

"That was nice of her," said Melanie.

"They did their jobs; that was their payment," explained Julia.

Melanie nodded, looking at the girls.

"Hey Jenn, Steph, have you ever been to the drive-in?" asked Krista.

"Like movies?" asked Stephanie.

"Right." Krista nodded.

"No!" they both answered in unison.

"Would you like to go with me tonight?"

"Yes!" both girls said, jumping up and down.

"*Beauty and the Beast* just happens to be on at the drive-in and I wanted to see it, but I'd look silly going without a kid. So would you two come with me? Of course your mom would have to come too," Krista said, glancing at Melanie with raised eyebrows.

"Can we, Mom? Oops. May we go to the drive-in?" Stephanie asked politely.

"I think that's a great idea," Melanie said, grinning at the girls and then at Krista. "Since it will be so late when we get back, why don't you spend the night with us, Krista?" Melanie asked.

"That sounds like fun!" said Julia, chuckling.

"Yeah, Krista. Spend the night with us! Please, please," said Jennifer, jumping up and down.

"Okay I will," she said, jumping up and down, making the girls laugh. "Do you want to come along with us, Jules?"

Julia feigned thinking it over and then smiled. "I think I'm going to pass, but maybe some other time."

"Okay. We'll tell you all about it," said Jennifer.

"Actually, Krista and I should probably get back to work now," she said.

"You're right. I'll see you tonight," she said to the girls and walked toward the door.

"I'll walk out with you," Melanie said, going with them.

When they were out of the cabin Julia turned to them and said, "Nice plan."

"It just came to me." Krista chuckled, giving Melanie a sideways glance. "I've been watching for something they could go see because I figured they hadn't been to the drive-in before. And it starts tonight."

"It just happens to end late so you could spend the night," Julia said playfully. "You don't need a reason, those girls would love it if you spent every night."

"That's true," said Melanie, linking her fingers through Krista's and squeezing.

They got in the pick-up and Melanie rested her hands on the window sill. She looked over at Julia and said, "Thanks for taking the girls into town with you."

"I had as much fun as they did. I'm glad to do it so y'all can have time together."

"I'll see you later," she said, kissing Krista quickly. She stepped back as Julia backed up and waved.

"God," Krista sighed. "I love her so much."

"I know." Julia chuckled.

"I swear Jules, I want to spend my life with her and the girls."

"Slow down, Krissy."

"Come on. You want the same thing with Heidi; you just won't admit it!"

"I do want that with Heidi and I want two girls just like Jenn and Steph. I'm going to name one of them Courtney."

"Oh you are! And what about the other one?" Krista laughed.

"I guess I'll let Heidi name her," Julia said, laughing with her.

"That seems fair." Krista sighed again. "I wish we didn't have to hide."

"I know. We won't always have to," Julia said. She glanced over at Krista. "I think I'm ready to tell my parents."

"Really?"

"Yeah. If they'd open their eyes I think they could figure it out with Heidi visiting."

"And the way y'all look at each other," Krista added.

"I can't help it!"

"I know! The same thing happens to me with Melanie!"

They laughed and got out of the pick-up. "I'll mow if you'll trim," said Krista.

"Deal."

* * *

Krista pulled up at the cabin freshly showered and ready for a fun night. She couldn't help smiling as she rounded the corner of the cabin and smacked right into Melanie.

"Whoa," she said as Melanie caught her and then pulled her close.

"Quick, babe, I need a kiss," Melanie said, bringing their lips together.

For a moment they stilled and let the softness of the kiss envelop them. Melanie pulled away and smiled. "I'm so glad you're here and staying," she whispered.

Krista returned her smile. "Oh what a night," she sang softly.

Melanie's eyes lit up. "Are you going to sing to me?"

"Someday." Krista giggled. "I got the music for the show in the mail today. That's one of the songs."

"Oh Kris, I cannot wait!"

They heard the back door slam and Stephanie yelled, "Krista's here!"

Melanie took Krista's bag and put her arm through hers and walked toward the cabin.

"This is going to be so much fun!" Stephanie said, putting her arm around Krista's waist.

"Wow, you'd think I never come to see you," Krista teased, loving the attention.

"Not to spend the night. It's like a slumber party!"

Krista laughed and put her arm around Stephanie as they walked into the cabin. She pulled Melanie aside and whispered in her ear. "I had no idea my heart could be this full."

Melanie looked at her with such love. "They can do that."

"It's not just them."

"I know," Melanie said, squeezing Krista's arm as she walked by and took her bag to the bedroom. When she came back Krista was sitting between the girls on the couch listening as they told her about their favorite characters in *Beauty and the Beast*. Melanie stopped and had to gather herself. It looked so natural for Krista to be there with them. This is what a family with two moms must look like, Melanie thought. *This could be our life. Couldn't it?* Before her imagination ran away from her Krista looked up and smiled at her. Then her face fell and her brow wrinkled.

Melanie quickly smiled at her and shook her head, indicating everything was fine. "My girls," she said, walking over and squeezing in next to Stephanie. She put her arm around her and rested her hand on Krista's shoulder. "I was thinking this might be a good night to go to McDonald's and then to the movie. What do y'all think?" she said, squeezing Krista's shoulder.

The girls looked at one another and then both said, "Yes!"

"Let's get our stuff together and go," Melanie said.

The girls jumped up and each grabbed a bag off the table with their snacks for the movie and ran to the car.

"Wow, you know how to clear a room, Mom." Krista chuckled.

She grabbed a bag of snacks she'd made for them and put her arms around Krista. "I love you, Kris," she said, her voice thick with emotion.

"I love you, too," Krista whispered back.

Melanie kissed her softly and was about to deepen the kiss when a horn blasted from outside.

Krista chuckled. "We'll finish this later."

Melanie rested her forehead on Krista's. "You can count on it."

14

They sat back and watched the girls on the playground at McDonald's like it was something they did every week. A couple of Krista's friends came in and she happily introduced Melanie to them. They chatted for a few minutes and then left. Thoughts of how normal this felt kept running through Melanie's head. No one was staring at them or whispering about them.

"You have such a contented look on your face," Krista remarked.

Melanie leaned over and said quietly, "I know. This all seems a bit surreal. We're sitting here watching our girls play just like any other couple would."

"You mean like that couple there?" Krista nodded behind them. "Or there?" she said, looking at the other side of the room.

"Yes. No one is looking at us funny. And," she said looking into Krista's eyes, "it feels incredible."

"I thought I was the only one thinking this," she whispered. "I mean, they are your girls, but it's like a peek into the future."

The girls came running up and said, "Watch me, Mommy! Watch me, Krista!"

"We're watching, sweetie," Melanie said, her eyes glistening. "Five more minutes." They both started to groan and Melanie added,

"Then the movie!" This stopped the groans and the girls ran off for one last round of play.

Melanie looked over at Krista as she clapped for both girls as they crawled through the play area and repeated what Krista had said, "A peek into the future." *Wouldn't it be nice.*

They waited in line at the drive-in and when it was their turn they paid and found a place to park. Krista checked the speaker to make sure it worked before turning off the engine.

"Okay, let's go to the restroom," Melanie said.

"I don't need to," said Jennifer.

"You know you will," said Krista.

Stephanie giggled. "You know she's right."

"After the bathroom we'll go to the concession stand for drinks and then it should be movie time," Krista said eagerly.

When they got back to the car Krista said, "Wait." She looked at Stephanie and Jennifer. "Your mom and I are taller and it will be hard for you to see from the backseat, so tonight you get to sit in the front and Mom and I will sit in the back. Okay?"

"Yes!" Stephanie yelled.

"Okay!" Jennifer parroted.

Melanie looked at her over the top of the car and nodded. "You think of everything, don't you?"

"I try." She winked.

They got in the back seat and got the girls settled in the front.

Melanie whispered into Krista's ear just as the previews started. "Is this like a date?"

It was dark in the car now and Krista took Melanie's hand knowing the girls couldn't see. "Yes, it's a family date."

"Just making sure because I want a goodnight kiss," whispered Melanie.

"Shh, you're not supposed to talk during the movie," Stephanie admonished them.

Krista grinned and whispered even lower, "You have all my kisses."

"Shhh," shushed Jennifer.

"Okay, okay!" Krista said loudly.

The girls giggled and they all settled in as the movie started. When it was over they switched seats and the girls quieted on the way back to the lake. Melanie turned to look at them and smiled.

"They're out. I thought they might fall asleep on the way back."

"What a fun night," Krista said.

"And the adult fun is just starting."

"You've got that right, momma," said Krista.

When they got to the cabin they each carried one of the girls inside.

"Just put her in bed," Melanie said, pulling the covers over Stephanie. "I made sure they were wearing comfy clothes because I thought they might fall asleep."

Krista laid Jennifer down gently and pulled the covers up. She kissed her forehead and then did the same to Stephanie as Melanie kissed Jennifer. She closed the door and they walked into the living room.

"Will they sleep all night?" asked Krista.

"Yeah. I got lucky, they are good sleepers and stay in their beds all night. They used to come in at night but thankfully they grew out of it."

Krista sat down on the couch and smiled. "This was so much fun. I didn't know I'd like it this much," she said, spreading her arms over the back of the couch.

Melanie walked over and crawled on top of Krista, straddling her. "I happen to know a few other things you like," she said, taking her shirt off and putting her hands on Krista's shoulders.

"Fuck," Krista whispered as her eyebrows shot up her forehead.

Melanie chuckled as she leaned down. "Exactly," she said, claiming Krista's lips and finishing the kiss from earlier. Her tongue invaded Krista's mouth, searching, and when it found Krista's, fireworks exploded inside her. "Mmm, that's what I need," she groaned.

Krista put her arms around Melanie and stood up. "We have too many clothes on," she said, leading them to the bedroom.

* * *

The next morning Krista held Melanie close as her head rested on her chest. "I love you, Mel," she whispered. "I wish we could wake up this way every morning."

"Oh sweetheart, so do I," Mel mumbled.

"I didn't think you were awake," Krista said.

"Do you remember when we were dancing at Jugs and you said you wanted to burn that moment into our memories?"

"Yes."

"I'm burning this moment there too." She raised up and looked into Krista's eyes. "No matter what happens Kris, we have this summer. And I intend to love you with all my heart and spend as much of it with you as possible. Okay?"

"Okay," Krista responded, her brow furrowed.

"If we start worrying about what happens at the end of the summer we won't be able to enjoy what we have. So let's keep making memories we'll have forever."

"I like that. I knew you were the smart one in this relationship," Krista said, kissing Mel's forehead.

"Don't ever sell yourself short, Krista. You're smart, too. Do you hear me?"

"Yes darlin', I do. Why so serious this morning?"

"We had such a good time last night and it won't be long until those girls will be up and ready for more. I love you so much and I don't want us to get caught up in looking ahead when we should be living in the now."

Krista smiled. "Then let's get up and make your sweet little girls their favorite waffles this morning."

"You remembered they love waffles," Melanie said affectionately.

"How can I not? They tell me nearly every day," Krista chuckled.

"You'd rather get up and make them waffles than stay in bed with me?" Melanie asked playfully.

Krista gazed at Melanie intensely and then said softly, "I wish that someday they'd come jump in bed with us and snuggle like one happy little family."

Melanie melted at Krista's sweet words. She caressed one side of her face. "Oh baby." She smiled. "Maybe someday."

"Until then," Krista said. "Let's surprise them with waffles."

Melanie nodded, bringing their lips together. This woman had taken her heart and made it new again. She'd never expected to fall in love and had planned to raise her girls on her own, but that all changed when Krista Kyle's eyes met hers. And it was obvious she loved Stephanie and Jennifer and they loved her back. Could they become a happy little family? Why not?

They got up and surprised the girls with waffles and spent the day laughing and playing. After McDonald's, plus the drive-in and waffles the next morning, the girls begged Krista to spend every night.

The week passed quickly and then it was time for the girls' extended visit with their dad. Krista planned to go with Melanie on Friday to take them to Dallas.

"Hey honey," Krista said to her at lunch on Thursday. "I was thinking that Julia could go with us to take the girls. After we dropped them off, we could meet Heidi at Jugs and do a little dancing."

"That sounds like fun."

"There will be a lot more people there, but we could still dance."

"Let's do it. I'd love to go dancing with you again," Melanie said, kissing her quickly as the girls played outside.

Krista didn't say anything and stared at Melanie, smiling.

"What?" Melanie asked.

"I love you, that's what."

15

After dropping the girls at their grandparents' house in Dallas, they met Heidi at a restaurant before going dancing. She hadn't been back to the lake since the weekend they went out on the boat. When she walked into the restaurant Julia's face lit up and she hugged her when she came to their booth. Heidi kissed her and then they sat down.

"Here we are together again," Heidi said. "It's good to see y'all."

They ordered and then caught up with one another.

"Are you ready for next Saturday's show?" Heidi asked Krista. "I was hoping to be able to come."

"I'm not ready yet, but I will be. I have the songs for the musical numbers and I've done the skits I'm in before."

"I'm not sure you'll have as much time as you think," said Julia, teasing.

"Why do you say that?" asked Krista.

"Because we just dropped the girls off. I think you'll be at the lake a lot this week."

"I think you should stay with me. That would make things much easier," Melanie commented, eyebrows raised, looking at Krista.

Krista chuckled. "I thought you'd never ask," she said, bumping shoulders with Melanie.

"I didn't think I had to ask," she said, kissing Krista on the cheek.

"That was brave," Krista said.

"I'm feeling brave tonight. The girls are happy with their grandparents, I'm out with my girl, and we're going dancing."

"Good for you," said Heidi. "Someday it won't take bravery. We can live our lives like anyone else."

"I can't wait, but I think for Krista and me, being back in our little town tends to closet us all over again."

"Maybe it would be easier if your families knew," said Heidi.

"I think I'm going to tell my parents at the end of the summer," said Julia. "That way if they freak out I'll be going right back to school."

Krista smiled. "Your parents aren't going to freak out. Now mine, that's a different story."

"I don't know, Krissy. They might surprise you."

Krista didn't say anything, but grabbed Melanie's hand under the table and pulled it into her lap.

"Won't they be at the show next Saturday?" asked Julia.

Krista nodded. "Oh yeah, they wouldn't miss it. I was hoping to introduce you to them. I mean, if you want to meet them," she said to Melanie, suddenly nervous.

Melanie smiled. "Of course I want to meet them."

"Her folks are really nice. They'll love you. After all, they love me," said Julia, laughing.

Before Krista could say anything their food came and the conversation moved to other things. When they finished eating, they headed to the bar. Julia rode with Heidi and on the way Melanie reached for Krista's hand.

"Are you nervous for me to meet your parents?"

"Not really. How do I explain this," Krista said, her face thoughtful. "I feel like I have you all to myself. Julia obviously knows, but no one else does."

"Are you ashamed or afraid?" Melanie asked.

"Not at all!" Krista said quickly. "I actually kind of hope some of my friends are at the bar tonight and I can introduce you. You did say I was your girl earlier, so I can introduce you as my girlfriend, right?"

"You'd better! I'm prepared to fight the women off you if I have to."

"Oh you are?" Krista laughed. "It will be the other way around, baby."

"I'm sure they'll get the idea when I'm kissing you on that dance floor," Melanie said boldly.

"Look at you! My girlfriend is getting all tough on me," Krista said, squeezing her hand. "I've got to say, I kind of like it."

Melanie laughed. "Hey, I meant what I said earlier. Will you stay with me at the cabin?"

Krista closed her eyes and held Melanie's hand to her heart.

"Are you okay?" Melanie said, glancing over at her.

"Yes, my heart just melted. We're going to a bar where we can be ourselves and we get to dance and then my gorgeous girlfriend asked me to stay with her for the next two weeks. It's like a little piece of heaven," Krista said, kissing the back of Melanie's hand.

"It is for me too, honey," Melanie said, pulling into the parking lot.

The bar was definitely more crowded than when they were there before. Julia slinked through the crowd and waved them to a table off to the side of the dance floor.

"Wow, it's electric in here," Melanie said, yelling over the music.

Krista grinned, nodding. "Do you want a drink?" she yelled.

"I'll get them," Heidi said as the music quieted.

"Thanks. How about a beer?" Krista said to Melanie. She nodded. Krista held up two fingers and Heidi disappeared into the crowd.

They sat down and Krista watched Melanie as she looked around people watching with a smile on her face.

"I can't believe it!" someone yelled from behind them.

Krista whipped around and smiled. "Hey Pam!" She stood and hugged the woman and turned to Melanie with a wide smile on her face. "This is my girlfriend, Melanie. Mel, this is Pam."

"Hi," Pam said, reaching out her hand.

"Hi, nice to meet you," Melanie said, shaking her hand.

"How's your summer going?" Pam asked.

Krista grinned and put her arm around Melanie as they sat down. "It's been the best!" Krista exclaimed.

Pam laughed and nodded. "I can see that. Cindy, Glenda, and Liz are sitting over there." She pointed toward the back of the room.

Krista nodded as the music began again. "Maybe we'll come over later. We've got some dancing to do."

"Have fun!" she said as they made their way to the dance floor.

Krista held Melanie's hand and pulled her onto the dance floor. She put her arms around her shoulders and yelled, "I love you!"

"I love you, too," Melanie yelled back. She pulled Krista close and kissed her possessively. Then she pushed her away, grabbing her hands and said, "Let's dance!"

The happiness on Krista's face lit the darkness of the dance floor. Overhead colored lights started blinking and the bass thumped through their bodies as they danced with abandon. After a couple of fast songs the beat slowed and Krista's arms were once again around Melanie. They began to sway to the music and Melanie's lips were next to Krista's ear.

"I love dancing with you. Can we do this every night when we get back to the lake?"

"I don't know. Does it come with kisses?" Krista said into her ear and then leaned back to look in her eyes.

Melanie's answer was a kiss that began soft and then she deepened it, forgetting where they were. They were lost in one another when the music changed once again to a lively beat that brought them both back to the bar.

"Sorry," she said to Krista shyly.

"Don't ever apologize for kissing me like that," Krista said, her eyes dark with desire. Then she smiled and grabbed Melanie's hand, pulling her toward the table.

They were sipping their beers when Julia came back to the table. "You may have to save me," she said to Krista.

"What's up?"

"One of those activists has Heidi's attention. You may have to go get her for me," Julia said, pointing to a table at the back of the room. "I'll lose her for the rest of the night if she talks to them for very long."

"Activists?" asked Melanie.

"Yeah, they're from the LGBT center. Heidi is going to be their volunteer legal advisor when she graduates."

Melanie watched as one of the women talked animatedly to Heidi. "She's passionate."

Krista eyed Melanie and said, "Are you interested?"

Melanie gave her a small smile. "I don't know. Maybe. I want the girls to be whatever and whoever they want to be. Things are certainly not equal now and they should be."

Krista smiled and before she could speak, someone sat in Heidi's empty chair. "Hey! So this is the reason you're not touring with us this summer," she said, nodding toward Melanie with a big grin on her face.

"Hi Liz," Krista said, putting her arm around Melanie protectively. "This is my girlfriend, Melanie. Babe, this is Liz. She'll be performing with me at the show next weekend."

"Hi Melanie, nice to meet you."

"Hi," Melanie said.

"Have you been rehearsing?"

"I'll be ready. Don't worry about me."

"I know you will." She looked at Melanie and smiled. "She's the star of the show. I'm sure she hasn't told you that."

Melanie looked at Krista affectionately. "I can't wait to see the show."

"I can't wait to sing to you," Krista said to her and winked.

"I can't blame you, Kyle. I'll see you next week. Nice to meet you," Liz said, getting up and walking away.

"What did she mean about you touring this summer?" Melanie asked Krista when Liz left.

Krista looked from Melanie to where Julia was watching Heidi.

"I'll explain later. Let me go get Heidi first. Okay?" She kissed Melanie quickly and left.

Melanie followed her with her eyes and then glanced at Julia. "What's this about touring?"

"Uh—well," Julia stammered. "Last summer they did the show at the lake and then they went to other places around Dallas and performed on the weekends."

"Are they doing that again?"

"I'm not sure," Julia said, obviously uncomfortable. "Krista will explain it."

"Julia?" she said. When she saw Krista walking her way with Heidi right behind her she let it go.

"There you are. Let's dance," Julia said, jumping up, grabbing Heidi's hand and pulling to the dance floor.

Krista looked on amused and sat down next to Melanie. "What was that?"

"She's running from me."

"From you?" Krista asked, confused.

"Yes. I asked her about this touring thing," said Melanie, pinning Krista with her eyes.

"Oh," Krista said, nodding. "It's not a big deal, babe. After next weekend's show they are going to perform it at four other venues on the following four Saturdays. I chose not to do it," Krista said, shrugging.

"Why? Don't you want to?"

"No," Krista said, taking Melanie's hand. "I don't."

"You did last summer."

Krista's brow wrinkled. "How did you know that?" Then Krista realized and added, "Oh, Julia. Yeah, I did it last summer, but I don't want to this summer. I have other things I want to do."

"Like what," Melanie said, narrowing her eyes.

Krista smiled seductively and leaned closer to Melanie. "Like spending every possible minute with you and the girls."

Melanie met her eyes and her heart melted. "Oh Kris, that's sweet, but this is your career we're talking about."

"This won't affect my career either way, Mel. It's a volunteer thing and I want to be with you and Steph and Jenn."

"But you'd do it if we hadn't met, wouldn't you?"

Krista shrugged. "Maybe. I don't know. It doesn't matter because we did meet and the only place I'm going is closer to you."

"What?"

"Why in the world would I want to leave on the weekends when I can be with you? Mel, you are where I want to be," Krista said earnestly. She stared into Melanie's eyes, hoping she could see the love in her heart. Her face softened into an enchanted smile. "Can we dance now and worry about my career later?"

Melanie stared at her and sighed. "God, this isn't good."

"What isn't?" Krista asked, alarmed.

"When you look at me like that..." Melanie said, not finishing her sentence.

"I'll have to remember that," she teased.

"Let's dance because I really need to kiss you right now," Melanie said, getting up and leading them to the dance floor.

They stayed for a while longer, knowing they had an hour drive back to the lake. Krista introduced Melanie to a few of her friends and they danced again and again. Later, Krista and Melanie got in the car and waited while Julia told Heidi good-bye.

Melanie took Krista's hand. "I'm glad you thought of this. I had such a good time dancing with you and we could sit at the table and hold hands or kiss and not worry about anyone staring or giving us a hard time. This is the way it should be for everyone."

"I've never had that much fun at the bar. We'll have to do it again. Okay?"

"Are you asking me on a date?" Melanie asked playfully, squeezing her hand.

"I am."

"Then I accept," she said happily.

"You accept what?" Julia said, getting into the back seat.

"We're going to do this again," said Melanie. "You and Heidi have to come too."

"You two were certainly the talk of the bar," said Julia.

"What?" Krista turned around to look at Julia. "I only knew a few people."

"Our friends and your theater buddies were talking about Krista's girlfriend," Julia said. "And how good y'all look together."

"Oh yeah?" Krista looked over at Melanie. "My girl is gorgeous," she said, grinning.

Melanie glanced over at Krista and chuckled. "Mine too."

Julia laughed. "Y'all are pretty people, that's for sure. I did hear Liz talking about you only doing one show this summer, though."

"It gives her a chance to be the star. Believe me, she's happy about it," explained Krista.

"She doesn't have as much talent as you do in your little finger," said Julia.

"Was she saying bad things about Krista?" asked Melanie, glancing in the rear view mirror at Julia.

"No. She was simply commenting that Krista's girlfriend was the reason she wasn't performing this summer."

"She's just jealous. And I'm lucky," Krista said, leaning over and kissing Melanie's cheek.

"I don't want to be the reason you don't do something you should, Kris. That's not good," Melanie said warily.

"It's not like that, babe. It's not required for school, it's volunteer. I'd rather be with you."

"Where are they? Maybe the girls and I could come watch."

"I've already told my professor I'm only doing the first show. There are several people that can't do them all. It's okay, but that's a nice idea."

"You know how much they wanted to be here to see you perform," said Melanie.

"I've already checked and they're recording it. Tim is sending me a tape for the girls."

Melanie glanced over at Krista. "If you're sure," she said hesitantly.

"Do you trust me?" Krista asked.

Melanie chuckled at the familiar question. "You know I do."

Krista smiled at her and gazed at her profile as the lights from the highway occasionally lit the inside of the car. There's no way she'd miss four weekends with this woman, she thought. She'd already been looking into schools near Houston. This summer had changed everything.

16

True to their word they danced every night, sometimes before dinner or before going to bed, and they always shared kisses.

"Do you have plans tomorrow night?" Krista asked as they held one another and danced to the slow rhythm coming from the radio.

Melanie pulled back to see Krista's face, thinking she was teasing. "Are you asking me out?"

"I am," said Krista. "I'll have to help unload Friday night when everyone gets here and then I'll be rehearsing Saturday most of the day. I thought tomorrow night we could do something special."

"I'd love to do whatever you have in mind tomorrow. Just so you know, every night we're together is special to me."

Krista smiled and wiggled her eyebrows. "It'll be fun."

"I thought you were supposed to be rehearsing this week, but I haven't heard you sing once."

"I have been rehearsing, just not here. I want it to be a surprise."

"I thought you'd be singing to me every night," Melanie said, pouting.

"Look at that face," Krista said, kissing her lips. "I'll sing to you. We're not doing this song, but It's one of my favorites." Krista put a tape in the player. She went back and put her arms on Melanie's hips and pulled her close.

The music to "Always and Forever" by Heat Wave began. Krista sang softly and held Melanie.

As the song continued Melanie couldn't stop the lump forming in her throat or the tears in her eyes. This was the most romantic thing that had ever happened to her. She could see the love in Krista's eyes and knew she meant every word, but on top of that Krista had the most beautiful voice she'd ever heard.

When the song ended, Krista said softly, "I love you, Mel."

"Oh Kris," Melanie whispered, cradling Krista's face in her hands. "I love you." She gently brought their lips together and kissed Krista with more passion than she'd ever felt before. This would be a memory she held dear for the rest of her life.

Not wanting this magically romantic moment to end, Melanie led them to the bedroom. They spoke in glances and touches at times breathless and then gasping. Slowly they undressed one another, Melanie took Krista's shirt off and then Krista did the same. In between wet kisses and nibbles the rest of their clothes came off.

Melanie took Krista's hand, kneeling on the bed, and nodded for Krista to do the same. Facing her, she ran her hands up Krista's arms and rested them over her shoulders. She looked into her eyes with such intense desire and love. Then she whispered, "Together."

She trailed her right hand down her chest, cupped her breast and ran her thumb over her nipple. Krista gasped and then did the same with her right hand. Melanie's eyes almost shut, but she wanted to see Krista's. She wanted to see every flash of heat to hunger to release to love. They didn't need words when their hearts were talking to one another like this.

Her hand snaked around and caressed Krista's bare cheek before coming forward to rest over her curly hairs. Krista's hand did the same and Melanie felt herself shudder with anticipation.

The corner of Krista's mouth twitched and her eyes narrowed slightly as Melanie parted her lips with her fingers, seeking her warm, thick wetness. She could hear Krista release a breath as she widened her legs, giving Melanie more room. As her finger circled, she could feel Krista's clit pulsating and then she trembled when Krista did the same to her.

Melanie had never felt so much love and desire. She wanted to touch and be touched at the same time and she could see this mirrored in Krista's eyes. It felt like she was seeing into Krista's soul. Maybe she hadn't known real love until this moment because her heart was full of Krista. She thought it might burst in her chest and if it did she imagined it would simply become one with Krista's.

That's what her heart wanted; to be with Krista. And it took over by guiding her fingers inside her lover. She could see the pleasure and joy fill Krista's eyes just as her fingers sought that perfect spot and connected. At the same time Krista found her quest inside Melanie and they melted together just as Melanie imagined. All they could do was hang on, their eyes never leaving the others, but then their lips met, seeking to do their part of cementing this bond.

Melanie had never felt anything like this. She was losing herself and finding herself all at the same time. It wasn't just giving all she had, but also receiving what Krista poured into her. She felt herself clench around Krista just as Krista grabbed her fingers from within. It was more than her fingers though. Krista was clutching and securing their love and together they locked it away for all time.

Their eyes met again as their bodies reached the pinnacle of this life shaping moment. Flexed muscles quaked and their skin quivered with euphoric sensation, but inside their souls exploded and the pieces whirred around in a spiral of love until it slammed into their hearts to remain always.

They crashed onto the bed, no longer able to support one another, gasping and heaving. This time when their eyes met the intensity had been replaced with a shared elation. Neither of them spoke; their hearts were still talking.

As they lay on their sides Melanie ran her fingers along Krista's cheek. Krista grabbed her wrist and kissed the palm of her hand. They both seemed to be struggling for words.

Melanie finally said, "I'll always remember the first time you sang to me."

Krista stared into Melanie's eyes and said earnestly, "I'll never be able to sing a love song without thinking of you."

Melanie pulled Krista into her arms and held tight, a sudden sense of foreboding niggling at the back of her mind. Surely something that felt this good and this right couldn't be undone.

* * *

The next day Krista was cleaning around the dock and unloading the boat that someone had recently returned from renting. She didn't hear Julia come up.

"What's wrong with you?" Julia said loudly. "I've been calling your name over and over."

"Oh hey, Jules. Sorry," Krista said.

"Are you okay?"

"Yeah, I can't seem to get Melanie off my mind."

Julia chuckled. "That's nothing new."

"Do you and Heidi talk about next year and beyond? Or is it understood that you're going to be together?"

"She told me that when she graduates she's staying in Dallas and already has a plan to get the job she wants."

"Have your plans changed after graduation? At one time you wanted to get as far away from Texas as you could. You haven't said anything about that lately."

"After things with Heidi became more serious my ideas changed."

"Don't you think Heidi would go with you if you still wanted to leave?"

"I don't know, maybe. That's just it. I don't want to leave now. I want to be where she is."

"Did you tell her that? Did y'all talk about it?" Krista asked.

"When she told me about the job she wanted she asked me if I'd be staying in Dallas. I asked her if she wanted me to and of course she does."

"So you both kind of assume?"

"We know we're both going to be there until I graduate in May, then we'll look ahead. Why all the questions, Krissy? What's going on?"

"I'm in love with Melanie, you know that. It all happened so fast and we agreed if we were worried about the end of the summer we wouldn't be able to enjoy this time we have. I've been planning to go to Hollywood as soon as I graduate, but now I feel differently about it."

"You feel differently how?"

"Like I don't want to go."

"What! You've been planning that for years!"

"There's no guarantee I'll make it, Jules."

"You have to try!"

"Do I?" Krista asked.

"Of course you do!"

"What if Melanie's next and not Hollywood?"

"Not Hollywood? You're going to be a star, Krissy! You will!"

"What if I don't want to be a star? What if I want to be with Melanie and the girls?"

Julia stared at her. "Do you hear yourself? Krista, you're in love. You can't let that cloud your judgement."

"Has being in love with Heidi clouded your judgement? You're willing to stay here. You said yourself that your ideas changed."

"But I'm not you. I'm a business woman with a brain for numbers and money. You're a star."

"What does that even mean, Julia? I'm no more important than you are."

"But you are," Julia said. "What's happened? Why are you thinking about this today?"

"We," Krista said hesitantly, searching for the right words. "It's hard to explain," she said shyly.

"You felt like you were exactly where you should be. Your soul found its home," Julia said quietly.

Krista looked at her wide eyed and slack jawed. "Exactly!"

"Here's the important part, Krissy. Did she feel it too?" Julia asked cautiously.

"Yes," Krista nodded. "I know she did. We didn't talk, there weren't words, but she felt it."

"I get it." Julia smiled. She looked at Krista thoughtfully and asked, "Can I say something, as your best friend, without you getting mad?"

"If you're going to say something about Melanie–" Krista started.

Julia held up her hands and said, "No, no. I like Melanie and can see how in love you two are."

"Okay. What?"

"It's a lot easier for Heidi and me because of where we are in life. It's not like that for you and Melanie. You have a career in Hollywood and she has kids, plus she's starting a new business," Julia said. She held up a hand so Krista wouldn't interrupt. "Hold on. You have obstacles that are a lot different than what we have. Please don't close your eyes to that and think that love can overcome it."

"I'm not." Krista sighed. "I know most people think we're still kids and I get that, Jules. I may be young, but that doesn't mean I don't know what I want. I'm a dreamer and always have been. In thirty years I'll still believe in love, I know that about myself. If for whatever reason Melanie and I can't make this work I know that I will never feel like I do now about anyone else. That's all there is to it. So why wouldn't I try to find a way to be with her the same as you will find a way to be with Heidi?"

Julia stared into Krista's eyes for several moments and then smiled. "You're right, so stop being so serious! Laugh, love, play and have amazing sex! You have all summer before any decisions have to be made."

Krista grinned. "Thanks Jules. This is the fucking best feeling ever, isn't it?"

"Yeah it is!" Julia agreed.

"I've got to get this finished," Krista said, jumping back in the boat. "I'm taking Mel out on the boat to watch the sunset. I'm trying to make it special since I'll be busy tomorrow and Saturday."

"I can't wait for her to see you perform. It's going to change everything," Julia said, helping Krista put the extra life jackets away.

"Why do you say that?"

"Because Krista, you may touch people's souls when you sing, but when you're on stage you take people to a magical place. It's incredible."

"Thanks Jules, but you're my biggest fan," Krista teased. "I sang to Melanie last night and I'm the one that was changed."

"What do you mean?"

"I sang a love song to someone I'm in love with. I'll always think of her when I sing about love now."

"That's kind of cool, Kris."

"Yeah it is. It feels a little strange, too."

Julia laughed. "I'll be watching you and Melanie when you sing Saturday. By the way, Heidi can't come after all."

"Damn. Sorry Jules."

"I'll sit with Melanie so she won't have to be alone."

"Oh thanks. I'll tell her."

"Okay, we're done here. What else do you have to do for this date?"

"I asked the restaurant to fix up something I could take on the boat."

"I'll go get it and put it in the boat for you. You go get your girl," said Julia.

"Thanks Jules," Krista said as they both left the dock and hit the walkway to the beach.

17

Krista gathered up what was left of their picnic supper and put it back in the bag. She opened a beer and handed it to Melanie where she sat in the back of the boat. Krista sat down next to her and they gazed out the front of the boat where the sun was sinking closer to the water.

"You have quite the romantic streak in you, Krista Kyle," Melanie said, squeezing her hand as she held it in her lap.

"I think it's you."

"Me? You planned this, sweetheart."

"What I mean is you make me want to do things like this. I love a beautiful sunset, but it's so much better with you," Krista said, leaning her head against Melanie's.

"I'm finding lots of things are better with you."

They sat in a comfortable silence and watched the sky continue to change colors as the sun slid into the water.

"So beautiful," Krista murmured.

"It is," Melanie agreed, looking away from the sky to find Krista looking at her. She chuckled, realizing Krista was referring to her. "You know what would make it almost perfect?"

"What's that?" Krista asked with a grin.

"If you sang to me again."

Krista had a thoughtful look on her face when she answered. "Maybe when we get back to the cabin."

Melanie smiled and turned to face Krista. With her finger under Krista's chin she guided their lips together for a gentle kiss. "Last night was incredible," she whispered.

"I'll never forget it," Krista said, looking deeply into Melanie's eyes.

"How about we do it again," Melanie said in a low voice.

"And again," Krista said, pressing her lips to Melanie's.

When the kiss ended she got up and pulled up the anchor wordlessly. Melanie made sure everything was secure in the boat and they motored back to the dock slowly in the twilight.

"Will I see you at all tomorrow?" Melanie asked as Bailey's came into view.

"Yes. I'll be over for lunch and I'll come by when I'm finished with work. I won't be too late after that."

"Okay." Melanie smiled. "I'm really looking forward to seeing you perform."

Krista smiled over at her. "I'm already nervous."

"What? I don't mean to make you nervous."

"I always get a little nervous, but I want to do my very best for you."

"Oh baby. You will."

They pulled up to the dock and secured the boat. Then they went back to Melanie's cabin.

"Thank you for a wonderful evening," Melanie said as they put their things on the kitchen counter.

"It's not over yet," Krista said, taking Melanie into her arms. She looked into Melanie's eyes and could see love. "I've never felt what I felt with you last night, Mel."

Melanie exhaled and cupped Krista's face. "I've never felt that either, Kris. It's hard to explain, but I could feel you everywhere. Around me, inside me, all over me; physically, mentally, in my soul."

"I know. I don't ever want to let that feeling go."

Melanie nodded. "Me neither."

Breathing a sigh of relief, Krista kissed Melanie softly. Then they walked to the bedroom hand in hand.

* * *

The next evening Melanie sat out on her beach after a swim. It was dark now, but Krista was true to her word. She'd been there for lunch today and had come by after work. Melanie sat back in her chair and looked up at the stars. Sometimes she wished she and the girls could stay here forever, but she knew that wasn't realistic.

Melanie was excited about starting her new business and the girls would be happy about school beginning again at the end of next month. But what about Krista? The last thing she'd expected to happen that summer was falling in love. A smile crossed her face; just thinking about Krista always made her happy.

She let her mind imagine a life with Krista, but not for long because was that realistic? But then again, now she couldn't see her life without Krista in it. She sighed and closed her eyes. Krista had already given up an opportunity to perform the rest of the summer to be here with her. She tried to play it down, but Melanie knew it was a big deal. Where could they go from here, though? Krista was off to Hollywood after she graduated next May.

This felt like so much more than a summer fling, Melanie thought. She knew Krista felt it too. It was like their souls had joined together never to let go. Is that the way it happened? She'd been in love, but it wasn't anything like this.

Then there were the girls. They adored Krista, but trying to make a life together would certainly affect them. *Am I brave enough to live with another woman as my partner and raise my children? What would that do to my new business? Would Krista want that?*

"So many questions," she said aloud softly.

"About what?" Krista asked, walking up and sitting down in Melanie's lap.

"Hey," Melanie said with a smile growing on her face. She hoped the darkness would hide the seriousness of the conversation she'd been having with herself.

Krista's eyes narrowed as she stared at Melanie then she leaned in and kissed her. "We'll figure it out," she said.

Melanie tilted her head and smiled as Krista read her thoughts. "How'd it go? Did you get everything unloaded?" she asked.

"We did. I start rehearsing in the morning, but I'll get a break at lunch. Oh, I forgot to tell you, Julia said she wanted to sit with you tomorrow night."

"Oh good. Do we bring chairs or sit on the grass?"

"People do both, but Julia has chairs for you."

Melanie smiled and held Krista's face. "I can't wait!" She kissed her with excitement and laughed.

"You have to because believe me, I need to rehearse, but right now," she said, getting up and taking Melanie's hand, "I need you more."

They walked up to the cabin and Krista stopped them at the back door. "I'll always need you," she said and kissed Melanie tenderly.

* * *

The next day was busy for Krista, but she managed to steal a few kisses between rehearsals and getting ready for the program.

Julia picked Melanie up in the golf cart and they set their chairs up early to get a good view of the small stage. They could see Krista behind the stage talking with her instructor and laughing with her cast mates. She must have felt their stares because she looked over, saw them and waved. After a moment she came over, smiling the whole way.

"Hey!" Melanie said, grinning.

"Oh my God," Krista said, her eyes wide. "I almost walked right up and kissed you."

"Good thing you stopped because I just saw your parents pull into the parking lot," Julia said.

"That might have been fun to explain," Krista said, chuckling. She reached over and squeezed Melanie's hand anyway.

Melanie looked at Krista and frowned. "Maybe it won't always be that way."

"It won't," Krista said firmly. "I wish I could kiss that frown off your face," she said quietly, leaning toward Melanie.

"Hey kids," Julia yelled and waved at Krista's parents. "We saved room for you."

"Here, let me help," Melanie said without thinking, walking over to take their chairs.

Krista followed her and took her dad's chair. "Mom, Dad, I'd like you to meet Melanie. Mel, these are my folks," she said, grinning.

"It's nice to meet you, Melanie," Krista's dad said. "You're not tired of this one yet?"

Melanie smiled. "Not at all. It's nice to meet you too, Mr. Kyle."

"Hello Melanie," Mrs. Kyle said. "I was hoping to meet your little girls. Krista can't stop talking about them."

"Nice to meet you, Mrs. Kyle. They are with their father this week, but they'd love to meet you when they get back," Melanie said.

"Krista needs to bring them in to swim at the city pool. I know they have the lake, but kids like the slide and the diving boards at the pool," said Mrs. Kyle.

"They would love that!" said Melanie.

"I'd be glad to take them," said Krista.

"We can fix hamburgers and hot dogs. You come too, Julia," Mr. Kyle said.

"You know I'm not going to miss one of your burgers," Julia said.

They set their chairs up next to Melanie and Julia's and Krista said, "Mel and Julia will take good care of you. I've to go. I'll see y'all after the show."

"Break a leg," her father said, grinning.

"Thanks Dad."

"I know you'll be wonderful, Krista. You always are," said her mother.

"Thanks Mom. I'm glad y'all are here."

Krista looked at Julia and Melanie and said, "I'll see you later."

"Break a leg." Julia winked.

Melanie smiled and was about to echo Julia's good luck wish when Krista said, "Walk with me."

She fell into step next to Krista and they stopped at the side of the stage. "In my head, I'll be singing to you all night." Melanie smiled. "But near the end I'm doing a Madonna song that's just for you."

"Okay, babe," she said softly. "Break a leg."

Krista smiled and took a deep breath. They locked eyes and said silent *I love you*'s with their hearts.

18

Melanie and Julia got everyone drinks from the concession stand and waited for the show to begin. Melanie quickly understood where Krista got her personality and kind heart. Her parents were warm and friendly and just as Krista had warned her, Mr. Kyle asked her plenty of questions. But she could see that he simply wanted to get to know her. They didn't seem concerned that Melanie was older than Krista and didn't think it was odd she was hanging out with a woman with kids.

"I'm glad Krista's staying here this summer and not touring with the group," Mrs. Kyle said.

"You are?" said Julia.

"Yes. Who knows when she'll get to spend a summer at home again?" she explained. "I know there are big things ahead of her."

"You're right," Julia agreed. "Once she hits Hollywood, we'll be lucky if she calls us."

"She won't do you like that, Julia," Mr. Kyle said.

"I know, but she's going to be busy," said Julia. She looked over at Melanie. "You'll know what we mean in a few minutes."

The show began and Melanie was immediately mesmerized by Krista. She was obviously the best one in the group and with good reason. Melanie knew Krista could sing, but this was incredible. She *was* a star!

After the first skit finished and before Krista and the band began to sing, Melanie leaned over to Julia and asked quietly, "Does she have any idea how good she is?"

Julia smiled. "Not a clue."

The band started a Whitney Houston medley, opening with "I Wanna Dance With Somebody." Krista smiled down at them and the audience couldn't help but nod their heads with the beat. They went straight into "I'm Your Baby Tonight" and Melanie felt like Krista was singing only to her as she strutted to the music and lyrics. The set ended with "Saving All My Love For You" and Melanie could feel tears stinging the back of her eyes.

Her heart swelled in her chest along with the tears as the realization hit her. The idea of her and Krista being together was only a dream. There was no way this talented woman would stay in Texas; nor should she. Melanie sighed, wiped the corner of her eyes and sat back, determined to enjoy the rest of the show. The talk they'd planned had just taken an even more dramatic turn, but that was for later. Right now, she planned to soak up all that Krista gave her because she was the one that Krista Kyle, star in the making, loved—and no one else knew that.

Julia leaned over and whispered in her ear, "It'll be all right."

Melanie looked over at her with surprise on her face.

"You'll find a way. Enjoy the show," she said with a compassionate smile.

Melanie nodded and the next skit was even better than the first. The crowd applauded as the actors exited the stage and the band returned.

This time they opened with Hootie and the Blowfish's "I Only Want to Be With You." The audience sang along and Krista had the happiest look on her face when her gaze settled on her parents, Julia, and then Melanie. They followed that song with Foreigner's "I Want To Know What Love Is." Krista's haunting voice brought tears to Melanie's eyes once again.

"Wow! She gets better and better," Mrs. Kyle said, applauding her daughter.

"Yeah she does," Julia agreed.

"She's incredible," Melanie added. Mrs. Kyle looked over at her with a proud smile.

The last skit began and Krista didn't have a part in this one. Melanie recognized her friends, Liz and Glenda, that she'd met at Jugs. They were good, but nothing like Krista.

The last song was the one Krista had told Melanie about. She could hear the first notes of the song and recognized Madonna's "I'm Crazy For You." Krista crooned the tune to the crowd, but looked over at Melanie often. She felt like Krista was giving her a gift that was only for her as the audience looked on, not knowing.

The song ended and the cast came out to take their bows to the appreciative applause from the crowd.

"That was incredible," Mr. Kyle said. "I know I always say that, but it was."

"I agree," said Mrs. Kyle. "What did you think, Melanie?"

Melanie had to quickly gather herself before she turned to Mrs. Kyle. "I'm awed. Krista is amazing."

Mrs. Kyle nodded. "She is."

"I knew she could sing, but my goodness, her acting."

"I thought you'd be surprised. I wanted to warn you, but you have to experience it." Julia laughed.

They waited for Krista after the show. She brought her professor over to meet her parents and Melanie. After a quick conversation she had to help load everything up and said she'd be back at the cabin as soon as she could.

Melanie and Julia walked Krista's parents to their car and they promised to get together when the girls returned.

Julia took Melanie back to her cabin in the golf cart and along the way she said, "I'm sure you're proud of Krista."

"Extremely proud," Melanie said.

"I don't know if you know this, but Krista has looked into schools near you and their drama programs."

"What?" Melanie exclaimed.

"I didn't think she'd told you yet. She will. I just happened to overhear her on a phone call or she wouldn't have told me.

"She only has one more year; she can't change schools."

"I think she'd do anything to keep y'all together. I know it's not my business, Melanie, but is that what you want?"

Melanie looked over at Julia. "More than anything, but there are so many things to consider."

"I get that, but you have a year."

"What do you mean?"

"She'll finish her degree in May; after that she's off to Hollywood. Houston is not that far from us, so you'll be able to see one another for now."

"I see what you're getting at. We haven't talked about what will happen after this summer, but we're going to this weekend."

"I'm here for both of you," Julia said, pulling into the driveway. "I want to help. Heidi will too."

Melanie smiled. "That's really nice, Julia."

"I've never seen Krista this happy and I've known her since kindergarten. Y'all are perfect together. But I know there's more to it. The girls, your career, Krista's career, oh and we can't forget the fact that we're gay. Someday that won't be a big deal, but for now it is."

Melanie sighed. "Tonight we celebrate my beautiful, extraordinarily talented girlfriend. We'll start on all the rest tomorrow."

"That is an excellent idea."

Lights shone on them from a car turning into the driveway.

"I think your extraordinarily talented girlfriend is here."

Melanie got out of the golf cart and shielded her eyes.

"Hey!" Krista said, getting out of her car.

"Great show!" Julia said, turning the golf cart around. "See y'all tomorrow!" she yelled and drove away.

Krista watched her and then looked at Melanie. "Why did she run off?"

"So I could do this," Melanie said, hugging Krista tightly. She loosened her grip and kissed Krista thoroughly. "You were amazing tonight," she said breathlessly.

"Wow! What a welcome," Krista said, catching her breath.

"All the women and men in that audience are wishing they could be me! They're all in love with you."

Krista laughed. "I don't think so. Can we go down by the water? I've got to wind down a little after that."

"Of course," Melanie said, taking Krista's hand. "Do you want me to get you a beer or something?"

"No," Krista said, putting her arm around Melanie. "All I need is you."

They went down to where the grass met the beach and plopped down on their backs and looked up at the stars.

Melanie propped on her elbow and looked down at Krista. "Do you have any idea how proud I am of you? You blew me away! Not to say that you don't usually do that in some way every day, but Krista, baby. You are so talented."

Krista grinned at the praise. "Thank you. It was so much fun seeing you in the audience right by my parents and Julia. *I* felt proud. The people that matter the most to me were right there, except for the girls," she said, looking over at Melanie.

"The girls are going to be screaming their heads off when they see the tape of this show."

They looked at the stars and enjoyed the quiet of the night for a few moments. Melanie glanced over at Krista and asked, "What are you thinking in that beautiful head of yours?"

Krista grinned. "Maybe someday I'll own this place and make it for lovers, just like you and me. They can come here and not worry about being found out. I could walk right up to you and kiss you like I wanted to earlier."

"I could see that happening someday. But you know what?"

Krista raised her eyebrows in a question.

"There's nobody around now and I could use one of your kisses."

Krista grinned. "I love you, Mel." She pulled her down on top of her and kissed her fiercely.

19

The next week flew by and Krista and Melanie spent as much time together as possible. They both missed the girls and were looking forward to picking them up the next day.

"This has been the best day," Krista said, her head resting on Melanie's chest.

Melanie giggled. "I can't believe we've been in this bed most of the day."

"It's a lazy Saturday," Krista said, sitting up. She leaned down and kissed Melanie softly. "Mmm, I could do that all day."

Melanie giggled again. "You have been doing that all day."

Krista laughed. "I guess I have."

"The girls come back tomorrow," Melanie said, stretching her arms overhead. "It's time to talk while we can, uninterrupted."

"Okay," Krista said, leaning against the headboard next to Melanie. "I think you know this, but I want to be sure. I love you, Mel," she said, smiling. "This can't end when the summer does. I know you have to go back to Houston and your business, and I have one more year in school."

"I don't want it to end either, Krista, but we have a lot to…" She paused. "Consider," she finished.

"I know. Number one are the girls."

"No. Number one is your school."

"I've looked into schools in your area," Krista started.

"Nope," Melanie interrupted her. "I've looked into schools too. Yours is the best for drama and you need to finish there. That's where you have the connection to Hollywood."

Krista looked down and then moved to face Melanie. "What if I don't want to go to Hollywood?"

Melanie smiled and said quietly, "You have to go to Hollywood."

"Why? I can do things with theater or even music in Houston."

"My sweet, baby girl," Melanie said, holding Krista's face. "You belong in Hollywood. You have to share this gift with the world. You wanted to before you met me and that shouldn't change."

"But–" Krista exclaimed.

"That doesn't mean we won't figure out some way to be together. Hollywood may be a bright, exciting mistress, but she can't take you away from me."

"Does that mean you and the girls will come with me?"

"I don't know about that. We have some things to figure out first. Like, what happens when we tell our families? I know you haven't come out to your parents yet and you'll be selective about that after you graduate."

"What about the girls? I don't want to hurt them and you know they'll get teased."

"I know, but I also know they are strong and they love you. I'm not sure how much they'll understand, but I'm explaining it to them eventually."

Krista nodded. "What do we do in the meantime? I still have to go back to school and you have to go home."

"I'm going to work my ass off to get this business up and going. That way we'll have more options when you graduate."

"I can come to you on weekends. You and the girls can come see me when we have a production. Julia and I have an apartment this year, so y'all can stay with us."

"We can work that so the girls can see their grandparents then, too."

Krista nodded and then stopped and looked at Melanie with a smile.

"What?" Melanie asked when she saw the smile on Krista's face.

"We're doing this." She grinned.

Melanie couldn't keep from smiling. "It's going to be hard, babe."

"I know that, but we can do it."

Melanie loved the optimism in Krista's eyes. She wanted to believe they could make it, but she knew there was no way she and the girls could follow Krista to Hollywood. That didn't mean they couldn't find a way though. They still had over a month of summer and then the hard part would start.

"I promise you that I will always try to make this work. There may be times when we'll be apart and it's hard to see a way through, but I'll always try," Melanie said with tears in her eyes. "But you have to promise me that you will not give up on Hollywood."

Krista stared at her but didn't say anything.

"Krista, I mean it. You gave up the rest of the summer to be with us. You can't do that with your future."

"What if my future isn't Hollywood?"

Melanie smiled. She could see the wheels turning in that gorgeous head. "It is and you know it. You have to try."

"But doesn't happiness count for something? If I'm in Hollywood but miserable, I'd much rather be happy with you and not be a fucking star. You all make so much of it," Krista said, irritated.

"You're getting angry and we're just talking about it. We're not there yet."

Krista sighed. "I'm not angry. It's just that everyone thinks I'm going to be this star and what if it doesn't happen?"

Melanie held out her arms. "You have a place right here and you will always be in my heart. You are my star."

Krista fell into her arms. "Then I'm not worrying about any of this until the time comes."

Melanie held her close. "I think that's a good idea."

Krista pulled back. "Let me get this straight." Melanie raised her eyebrows and smirked.

Krista chuckled. "You know what I mean. We'll take turns seeing one another this year." Melanie nodded. "My phone bill is going up." Krista laughed.

"You didn't promise me, Kris," Melanie said seriously.

"I promise to do whatever it takes for us to be together," Krista said.

"No!" Melanie said forcefully.

"I promise to go to Hollywood and do my best."

"That's my girl. We'll have our time."

"Our time? When we live together as a family?" asked Krista.

"Won't that be wonderful," Melanie said, pulling Krista to her and stroking her back. "My soul has found the one it loves," she said softly.

"Our souls, we'll always be connected, Mel. Ours is a never ending love story." Krista pulled away to look into the eyes of the woman she loved. She could see Melanie's love shining back at her. Their lips met once again, sealing their promises to one another.

20

P resent Day

Stephanie and Jennifer looked at Krista and Melanie as they ended the story of how their love began.

"We made it that next year just as you planned," said Stephanie. "We remember visits to your apartment with Julia and seeing your shows." She looked over at Julia and then back to Krista.

"When we left here, I was concerned with how all of this would affect you girls. I didn't want you to be bullied or teased and I thought you might be too young to understand," Melanie said and then she looked at Krista. "But I was so in love with you and desperately wanted to make it work."

Krista smiled at Melanie but before she could say anything Jennifer said, "You were worried about us? We loved Krista too!"

"When we left here I was concerned about the girls too," Krista said, smiling sadly at Melanie. "And I had it in my head that I would keep my promise to you and go to Hollywood, but then I was moving to Houston as fast as I could."

"I knew that's what you were thinking," Melanie said, narrowing her eyes at Krista.

Krista grinned. "You said you wanted honesty and the things that were unsaid."

"I can't believe you didn't think we could handle it!" said Stephanie sharply.

"It was a different time," Melanie calmly replied.

"I wasn't out. How could your mom start a new company with a woman living with her and her two young daughters?" Krista said, defending Melanie.

"Bullshit! Don't tell me appearances mattered!" said Jennifer.

"I told you they were going to be upset," Krista said to Melanie.

"I know," Melanie said softly.

"It doesn't matter as much now, but it did then," Heidi said.

"That's right. Heidi was the only one that was out then," added Julia.

"When we were all together I could believe it would all work out," said Krista, smiling. "It was so good, but then I'd have to go back to Dallas or y'all would have to go back to Houston and I missed you terribly."

"Hell, I even missed y'all," said Julia, lightening the moment.

"What happened after you went to Hollywood?" asked Stephanie.

"I did a few auditions and had a few call backs. I got a couple of commercials and had a bit part in a TV drama. Then I came to Houston at the end of the summer, planning to move there," began Krista.

"But," Melanie said, "I wouldn't let her move." She looked into the fire.

"Why not!" Stephanie exclaimed.

"Because she was trying to get the business going and at the same time give you two a good life," Krista said with frustration in her voice. "Believe me girls—I know you're not girls anymore," she said apologetically, shaking her head. This got a smile from Stephanie and Jennifer. "Believe me," she repeated calmly. "We wanted to be together, but times were different and we were in Texas. Even in Hollywood it could have been career suicide at that time." She exhaled loudly and shook her head again. "Your mom and I managed to fuck up everything."

"That's not quite fair," Heidi said quietly.

Krista and Melanie both looked at her.

"You had so many obstacles to navigate unlike Julia and me. You did the best you could at the time," she said.

"I don't know about that," said Melanie. She turned to Krista and took her hand. "I owe you the biggest apology, Kris. I should have never said no to you. I've been sorry every day of my life that I didn't let you move to Houston," she said with tears in her eyes.

"No!" Krista said. "You were doing what we *both* thought was right at the time." Then a wistful smile crept onto her face and she added, "However, when I look back and play the 'what if' game, I always go back to that time and wonder what would've happened if I'd been brave enough and moved to Houston anyway."

"That's just it though," Julia spoke up. "You could've moved there and everything could have fallen apart and you wouldn't be the family you are today."

Krista smiled at her friend and then squeezed Melanie's hand. "I remember the times when we were all together, I felt like the girls were mine too. We were a family." Tears fell onto her cheeks and she quickly brushed them away. "No offense to your dad," she said to Stephanie and Jennifer.

"That's another obstacle you had," said Heidi. "I remember when we talked about what he could do as far as custody went."

Krista and Melanie looked at one another with sad faces and nodded.

"Oh wow, I didn't even think about that," said Jennifer. "Dad might have given you trouble. It took him a while to come around when Stephanie came out."

"Wait a minute, what happened after you went back to Hollywood? Did y'all break up? I mean, you wrote to us, you called us, you were still in our lives. We just didn't see you as often."

"I guess you could call that the next fuck-up," said Krista.

Melanie shook her head and looked down at their hands. "We hadn't seen each other in over a year. We called and wrote letters, but it was hard. You were busy by then too."

Krista nodded. "That's when I'd just gotten the sitcom part."

"I didn't want Krista to be as miserable as I was, so I told her we were through. I thought I was being this good person, letting her go. Until you met Tara."

Krista grinned. "You didn't feel like such a good person then, did you?"

"No, but I faked it, didn't I?"

"Yeah you did," Krista said and they both laughed. "Tara was very attentive, to say the least," said Krista. "Long story short, we fell in love and life was great. Until it wasn't. We were together several years and she was more established in her career. She was tired of hiding and wanted to come out, but I wasn't ready. We held on for a year or so after that and she came out anyway. So that was the end of that."

"That's terrible!" said Stephanie.

"It was at the time, but not really. She was ready to live her life and be her authentic self. I was too afraid my career would suffer. She is one of my best friends now." Krista took Melanie's hand. "Your mom came to Hollywood to mend my broken heart," she said, smiling.

"And that was the next fuck-up." Melanie smiled back at her and squeezed her hand.

"What happened then?" Stephanie said, exasperated.

"I know," Heather, who had been sitting quietly watching the dynamic between Krista and Melanie, said quietly.

Krista looked at her and smiled.

"That's about the time Stephanie came out and had problems in college. Am I right?"

Melanie nodded. "I did go out to Hollywood and stayed for a

week. You were already over Tara; it had been several months since she'd come out."

"We had such a good time," Krista said, tilting her head with a dreamy look in her eyes.

"Yeah we did," Melanie said softly.

"Oh no. It was my fault," Stephanie said with horror in her voice. "That's when you became an activist. I'm the reason you're not together."

"It's not your fault," insisted Krista. "Your mom wanted to be an activist from the first time she met Heidi's friends at the bar all those years ago. She talked about it for years before she actually had the time to do it."

"But you weren't out yet, so you couldn't really be around Mom and her loudness," Jennifer said, holding her hands up and waving them in a circle.

"It's so easy to look back and say I should have done that, isn't it? Maybe if I would've come out then we would still be together today," said Krista.

"You don't know that," Melanie said with kindness in her voice.

Krista smirked. "You know it as well as I do. Once again, if I'd only had courage."

"Then why didn't you come get Mom when you came out?" asked Stephanie.

"That would be fuck-up number 435," Krista deadpanned.

"Not at all," said Julia. "You were in the middle of being America's favorite mom on your next successful sitcom and Melanie's company was about to go international. There's no way either of you could have moved or even had time for each other."

"Really? I don't think so. We should've found a way. It's all timing with us. This is a never-ending story because it's never going to be our time," Krista said, frustrated. "I need something to drink." She walked over to the ice chest on the patio by the back door.

Stephanie jumped up and followed Krista to the patio. She grabbed her hands and said with tears in her eyes, "Krista, please don't give up on us. Please don't give up on our family."

Krista's face softened and she took Stephanie in her arms and hugged her. "I'm not giving up on our family. I've never done that and never will."

Jennifer walked up and put her arms around both of them. "We'll always be a family. A little different, but a family."

"I'm sorry you and Mom had such a hard time. I'm sorry we didn't seem strong enough," said Stephanie.

"What? That didn't matter. It was us not wanting to put that on you. If I'm being honest, I think we were both afraid. Not just for you two, but afraid of coming out," Krista said.

"But what about now? You need to talk to Mom. Things have changed; that's one reason we're here," said Stephanie.

"You mean we're not going to celebrate your birthday?" Krista said, her eyebrows raised.

"That's one thing we're celebrating, but," Jennifer said, choosing her words carefully, "there's another. Talk to Mom."

The screen door flew open and Kyle, followed by his sister and cousins, came bounding out of the cabin. "The movie is over," he yelled, running up to his mom. "Can we watch another one?"

Stephanie looked at Krista and then at Jennifer. "Go ask Momma and let's see what she thinks, okay?" she said, smiling down at her son.

"Okay," he said, running to Heather.

Krista watched him and felt such love in her heart, but it also felt weary. "You know, I think I've had enough reminiscing for one night," Krista said, looking at Stephanie and Jennifer.

"I'm sure it's not helping your heart," said Jennifer.

"You'd know about that, wouldn't you?" Krista said compassionately.

"I do. Divorce is hard. I know you weren't married, but it's similar. I don't care how amicable it is. It hurts and it takes time for your heart to heal."

"Has your heart healed?" asked Krista.

A small smile crept on Jennifer's face. "It's getting there."

Krista nodded and turned to Stephanie. "I'm speaking for us

both," she said, glancing at Jennifer. "We don't want you to ever experience it."

Stephanie nodded. "We've all had break-ups and I know I've never had anything as severe as what you both have been through." She paused and looked over to where Heather was talking to both their children. "We vowed to always work on our marriage and so far so good."

Melanie walked up to them and put her hand on Krista's forearm. "Are you okay?"

Krista smiled. "Yeah, are you?"

"Not really. I knew this would be hard."

"We're really glad you told us," Stephanie said gratefully.

"I wanted you to know why Krista is so special to our family," Melanie said, staring into Krista's eyes.

Krista smiled as Julia and Heidi joined them.

"Hey, we're going to head home now. See you tomorrow?"

"Yes, I need your help. Melanie wants to take everyone to the cliffs," Krista said. "We'll need both boats."

"I'll try to talk this one into taking a day off," Julia said, elbowing Heidi.

"Oh, that would be great!" said Melanie. "It'll be like old times."

"Do you think we can get Krista to sing?" asked Heidi.

"Only if you all join me," Krista said, chuckling.

"Thank y'all for being here tonight," said Melanie, hugging them both.

Julia and Heidi nodded, then Julia met Krista's eyes and said, "See you tomorrow."

Krista nodded and assured Julia she was okay with a look.

When they walked away, Melanie turned to Krista. "Can I walk you home?" She realized what she'd said then added, "I mean, walk you to your cabin?"

Krista gazed at her for a moment and then said, "I'd like that."

21

Stephanie and Jennifer watched their Mom and Krista walk away. They bumped shoulders as they saw their mom put her hand in Krista's.

"Come on kids," Heather said. "It's bedtime."

"Slumber party for the cousins in our cabin," said Jennifer.

"Are you sure?" said Stephanie.

"Yep. You and Heather should have a little fun in your cabin the same way Mom and Krista did," she said, wiggling her eyebrows up and down.

"Let's get your PJ's on," Heather said, mouthing 'thank you' to Jennifer as she walked by.

"I hope they can figure this out. They belong together," said Stephanie as her mom and Krista disappeared down the road.

"I hope Mom is patient. If Krista's heart feels anything like mine did, it's numb. You feel love for your kids and family, but to even think about romantic love—there's just nothing there."

"Mom has made up her mind. And you know she gets what she wants. I think the waiting is over. Their time is here and now," said Stephanie.

"She has done everything she can to show Krista that. I hope she tells her about it tonight."

"Me too! I wanted to tell her as soon as we saw her, but that's Mom's story to tell."

"I can't wait to call Krista 'Mom' because I know they're going to make it this time," Jennifer said, looking at her sister.

Stephanie chuckled. "She'll be speechless."

"Yep."

They went inside, still chuckling.

* * *

Melanie slid her fingers into Krista's hand like she'd done so many times before.

"I always loved holding your hand," Krista said as they walked up the path.

"I still do."

They walked along in silence enjoying the quiet.

"Could we go sit on the dock?" asked Melanie.

"Sure."

They strolled up the walkway until they reached the end of the dock then slid their sandals off and skimmed their toes over the water.

"This reminds me of skinny dipping," Melanie said.

"Do you want to?" Krista asked, looking over at Melanie. She could see her eyes sparkling in the moonlight just as they had the first time they went skinny dipping.

"I'm not as bold as I was then as far as my naked body goes. You do remember that I'm twelve years older than you," Melanie reminded her.

Krista chuckled. "That always bothered you, but not me."

"Those twelve years make a big difference with the wrinkles and other unsightly things that happen as we age," Melanie said, bumping her shoulder against Krista's.

"Mel, you know that you are always the most beautiful woman to me because I *see* you. I see inside to the most beautiful parts of you."

Melanie gazed into those blue eyes that always felt like home. "You always see me, Kris."

Krista smiled at her and they simply enjoyed gazing into one another's eyes for a few moments.

Melanie broke their stare and said, "You said that we should have found a way to be together. I've done some things to make that possible."

"What do you mean?" Krista asked, her brow furrowed.

"I've been ready to turn the business over to the girls and almost did five years ago. But I realized I'd let the business come between us more than once and I was afraid that might happen to the girls. I've been waiting until I was sure they had the right balance in their lives that we could never seem to find."

Krista patiently waited for Melanie to go on.

"I was about to begin the process of turning my clients over to them when you called and told me about Brooke."

"What?"

"I feel responsible for your heartache, Kris. Honestly, I feel responsible for all your heartaches because most of them happened in one way or another because of me."

"That's not true, Mel. I'm telling you, the world, fate, karma—whatever you want to call it—has finally gotten through to me. I'm supposed to be alone. That's it."

"No it's not. You wouldn't have fallen for Brooke if I'd have trusted myself and done what I'd planned to do. We would have been together. You and Julia would still have bought this place and you would have still helped Brooke. But you wouldn't have fallen in love and gotten your heart broken again."

Krista shook her head. "What are you talking about?'

"Think back to five years ago. If I would've come to you then we could've been together."

Krista thought back and then gasped. "That's when Kyle was born. We saw each other at Stephanie's."

"Exactly. I wanted to tell you I'd come to LA, that it was our time, but I waited and before I knew it you called me and told me about Brooke."

"What did you mean I would've helped Brooke anyway?"

"Your heart is as big as Texas," Melanie said, chuckling. "You want to help people. That's one reason you and Julia created Lovers Landing. You would have still helped Brooke find herself, but you wouldn't have fallen in love with her. And you would have found her first love and probably set them up."

Krista looked out over the water and considered Melanie's words.

"I don't mean to be harsh, babe," Melanie said.

Krista looked over at her hearing the familiar term of endearment. "Harsh?"

"Yeah. You and Brooke didn't belong together. I'm sure you got caught up in the romance of this beautiful place and you were lonely."

Krista knew that most of what Melanie said was true. "Tell me something, Mel. Why didn't you ever call me about people you dated over the years?"

Melanie smiled. "Because there weren't any. When you were with Tara I tried. I went out with a fellow financial planner once, but could tell immediately it was a mistake. And then I went out a couple of times with one of the other mothers in Stephanie's class."

Krista raised her eyebrows.

"She was 'experimenting,' as they say," Melanie said, making air quotes. "I could see that you were the only person my heart would ever be happy with. Of course I knew that because our souls have been one since our secret summer in 1991."

Krista rubbed her hands over her face. *Why do we keep screwing this up*, she thought.

Melanie grabbed Krista's hands and turned toward her. "When Stephanie showed me that news clip of your break-up my heart stopped. I was so sad for you and almost called you right then, but I knew you needed time. So I called Julia instead."

"What?"

"I've been talking to Julia every few days for months. I made her promise not to tell you, so please don't be upset with her."

"Okay..."

"I knew you needed some time, so I went to work. I've transferred all my clients to the girls and my only client now is you. As of last week, I sold my house."

"You what?"

"Yeah, I'm done, Kris. It's our time."

Krista's stomach fell and her heart thumped in her chest. With tears in her eyes she said, "My heart isn't worth having, Melanie."

"I know your heart, baby," Melanie said, squeezing her hands.

"I won't risk it. I won't risk our family. Imagine what would happen if we don't make it, Mel."

"That's not going to happen. You once told me I was looking at the wrong things, now you are. Imagine what would happen when we're together. Imagine the love and happiness in our family."

Krista shook her head. "It's too much to risk," she whispered.

"Okay. Do you trust me, Kris?"

"That's not fair, Mel!" Krista said, protesting.

"Hold on," she said, still grasping Krista's hands. "You were the one romancing me back then. You said I made you want to be romantic. Remember?" Krista nodded. "It's my turn. Let me romance you and I'll help you find the courage you spoke of earlier. Because I've found mine."

Krista was so conflicted. She had always wanted to be with Melanie more than anything. But she pushed those feelings down because at least she had her relationship with the girls and now the kids. They could never overcome whatever obstacle stood between them and now Melanie was saying this is it. There was nothing in the way. No business, no closet, no careers to worry about. Krista wanted to believe her, but she'd been hurt so many times.

"I don't think I'm strong enough," Krista said with tears in her eyes.

Melanie gave her the sweetest smile. "That's why I'm here. I am your strength."

Krista stared into her eyes, searching for clarity. She knew Melanie never *wanted* to hurt her, but they had hurt each other over and over. She knew she wouldn't survive if it happened again.

"Let me show you. One day at a time," Melanie said, her eyes full of hope.

Krista released the breath she'd been holding. She could give her tomorrow and see how it went. Then if her heart felt better, she'd give her the next day. *One day at a time*, she repeated over and over in her head.

Krista took a deep breath and exhaled once again. "I'll give you tomorrow," she said softly.

The most beautiful smile grew on Melanie's face.

22

Melanie walked up to Krista and kissed her on the cheek. "Good morning. Did you sleep well?" she asked cheerily.

Krista narrowed her eyes and couldn't stop the grin that appeared on her face. "How do you do that?"

"Do what?" Melanie said innocently, still holding one of Krista's hands.

"Know the answer before you ask the question." She chuckled. "For your information, I slept better than I have in a long time."

"Oh good," Melanie said, obviously pleased. "Wonder why," she murmured. "I on the other hand did not sleep much."

"Why?" Krista asked, concerned.

"I got booted out of my cabin and sent to the cousins slumber party."

"The what?"

"When I walked you home Jenny decided to throw a slumber party for the cousins. I think she said Stephanie and Heather were going to have a little fun in our old cabin. So I was the lucky Mimi that got to help chaperone a movie marathon," she explained as they walked over to the others. She leaned over near Krista's ear and said, "I may want to stay with you tonight so I can sleep."

Krista giggled, thinking that there wouldn't be much sleeping going on if Melanie stayed with her. Then she realized that was the first time she'd even thought about sex in months.

After Brooke left, Krista had looked back at their relationship and found she'd missed several signs of trouble because they were so busy with the award season. At the beginning their sex life was healthy and plentiful, but the last year had been anything but. She shook those thoughts out of her head when Kyle grabbed her leg in a hug.

"Kwista," he said with his adorable little lisp. "Mommy says I'm named after you, but my name isn't Kwista," he said seriously.

Krista rubbed her hand through his dark locks and asked, "What is your whole name?"

He stood a little straighter and said clearly, "Kyle Zimmer-Lopez."

"Right," Krista said, nodding. "Do you know what my whole name is?"

He looked up at her with the most beautiful dark brown eyes and shook his head.

"It's Krista Kyle," she said, emphasizing her last name.

"What!" he said, realization showing all over his face. "I *am* named after you!"

Ava was listening to this unfold and rolled her eyes. "I tried to explain it to him."

"I'm sure you did." Krista surveyed the group and said loudly, "Julia is waiting on us at the dock. Who wants to ride with Mimi and me in the golf cart?"

The four third-generation Zimmers ran to the golf cart. Krista and Melanie laughed as they turned and watched them go.

Melanie put her arm around Krista's shoulders as they began to follow the kids. "How does your heart feel now?" she asked.

Krista put her arm around Melanie's waist and said quietly so the kids couldn't hear, "Pretty fucking good."

Melanie threw her head back and laughed loudly.

Krista looked over her shoulder and said, "Are y'all coming?"

Stephanie answered sarcastically, "Thanks for thinking of us. We did make those bundles of joy, you know."

Krista threw her hand up and waved with her back to them. "Toodles."

When they got to the golf cart Kyle was behind the wheel pretending to drive.

"Oh, I don't think so," said Krista playfully. "In the back seat, I need Mason on one side, Preston on the other with Ava in the middle," Krista barked orders and the kids jumped to their seats.

She picked Kyle up and had him stand next to the golf cart while she and Melanie got in the front seat.

He looked at her and waited.

"I guess you're going to have to sit on my lap, Kyle," she said with a twinkle in her eye. She got him settled and then added, "Would you help me drive?"

"Yes ma'am," he said, full of glee.

Krista turned to look at the kids in the back. "Don't worry, everyone will get a turn." She winked. She was rewarded three wide-eyed grins on excited faces. When she hit the gas pedal she could feel Melanie's hand pat her shoulder as she rested her arm across the back of the seat.

When they pulled up to the dock, the kids ran up the walkway to where Julia and Heidi were waiting with the boats.

"They are so excited," Krista said, getting out of the golf cart and waiting for Melanie.

"So am I. You're giving me today, right?" Melanie asked, placing her hands on Krista's shoulders.

"All day long," Krista promised.

"Thank you," Melanie said, taking Krista's face in her hands and kissing her quickly.

It surprised Krista, but it also pleased her because it was the most natural thing for Melanie to do. Her heart lurched, but she noticed it was in a good way, not full of pain like it had been the last several months.

"You okay?" Melanie said, searching her eyes.

"Such a rushed kiss?" she said with a playful glint in her eyes.

Melanie gave her a hint of a smile and said earnestly, "I don't want to overwhelm you."

Krista could see the concern and uncertainty in Melanie's eyes, but she could also see the love that had always been there. "I trust you, Mel."

The smile grew on her face until it reached her eyes.

About that time the other golf cart pulled up. Stephanie, Jennifer and Heather got out and simply walked past them, all smiles.

Heather stopped Stephanie and gave her a quick kiss. She turned and said, "What a beautiful day."

"Yeah it is," agreed Melanie and they all headed for the boats. The air was full of giggles, laughter, and everyone talking at once.

"Mimi and I want Kyle, Preston, Stephanie and Heather in our boat," Krista said, walking up to the group.

"Then the rest of you'd better get in with Heidi and me because we're going to beat them to the cliffs," Julia said, laughing.

"Our boat, huh?" Melanie murmured to Krista.

A hint of a smile played at the corner of Krista's mouth as she shrugged.

As everyone got settled and put life jackets on the kids, Krista looked at Stephanie and Heather and said, "I need to know one thing."

"What's that?" Heather said.

"When you walk into the back door of the cabin you're in the kitchen and then you walk to the left into the living room. Right?"

"Yeah," Stephaine said, bewildered.

"Then when you get to the hall the first door on the left is a bedroom. Please tell me that's where you're staying because I heard about the slumber party last night."

Heather grinned. "That is our room. Why?"

"Whew," Krista said loudly, running her hand over her forehead. "Because that's *not* my bedroom."

Melanie was standing behind Krista and whispered in her ear,

"Don't worry, babe. There's no way I'd let them mess up our big queer energy. I'm sleeping in our room and I can still feel you there."

Krista turned her head so she could see Melanie's eyes and could've lost herself in them.

"Mimi, you said it's not nice to whisper and tell secrets when other people are around," Kyle reprimanded her.

"I sure did, honey. Sorry about that. Do you have your life jacket on?"

"Yep."

"Come on, you can sit with me across from Krista," Melanie said.

Krista started the motor and Heather untied them from the dock and pushed them away. They slowly puttered along in the cove and Krista turned to see Preston sitting between Stephanie and Heather in the back. Stephanie was pointing to different places telling him about when she was here as an eight-year-old.

She looked over at Melanie and found her holding Kyle tight and smiling at her. It took her back thirty years to when they were in the boat and Melanie would look at her the same way, her eyes full of wonder and ready for whatever came next.

Krista couldn't help smiling back at her. "Is everyone set? We've got to catch them," she said, pushing the throttle down. The boat took off over the water. She heard the cheers and whoops as they pulled up alongside the other boat.

They got to the cliffs and tied the boats together and dropped anchor.

Melanie looked up at the cliffs and said, "Wow, this brings back memories. Do you remember, girls?"

Jennifer laughed. "I remember jumping in and you were so proud of me. You acted like you were afraid and I'd really done something."

Krista chuckled. "That wasn't an act."

"What?" Jennifer exclaimed.

"I had to jump after you did. I really was afraid," Melanie said, laughing.

"Wow!" said Jennifer. "Let's go, Mom! I'll jump with you."

They jumped in and swam over to the natural rock shelf that

acted as steps to the taller cliffs. The boys followed them and Krista looked on with Ava and Kyle.

"Watch how they step on the rocks and then crawl out of the water onto the shore. Then you walk up to where you want to jump off."

They both nodded and Krista could see Ava watching carefully, working through any fear. Kyle snuck his hand inside hers and watched his grandmother and aunt step onto a rock and face the boat.

Krista smiled and kneeled and told him, "See how they're smiling. It's fun. Watch." Krista stood and yelled, "Mimi, wave at us!"

Melanie heard her and waved at the others. "Here we go!" She looked over at Jennifer and nodded. They both stepped off the cliff and splashed into the water after whoops and cheers.

"See! Do you want to try it?" Krista asked Ava and Kyle.

"I do," said Ava. "Will you go with me, Mommy?"

Stephanie was already in the water and held her arms out for Ava to jump. "Come on, baby. I'll go with you."

Ava jumped in and Krista looked at Kyle. "Do you want to swim, Kyle? You don't have to jump if you don't want to."

He looked up at Krista. "Will you swim with me?"

"Yes, let's go."

They got in the water and watched the others jump. Ava and Stephanie jumped in holding hands. Heather jumped in and swam over to Krista and Kyle.

"Do you want to jump, buddy?" asked Heather.

"Not yet, Momma. I'm swimming with Kwista."

"Okay. When you're ready I'll jump with you."

Kyle nodded.

Heather looked at Krista and said, "All good?"

"Yep," said Krista. "We're having fun."

Heather swam away and joined the others jumping.

Melanie jumped again and then swam over to them, grinning at Krista. "Did you ever think we'd be doing this with the grandkids?" she asked, her voice full of happiness.

Krista laughed. "No. And even if I had it wouldn't be this wonderful."

Melanie held on to Krista and Kyle since she didn't have on a life jacket. Krista couldn't help but feel all this love and once again felt like the kids and grandkids were hers too. The joy almost overwhelmed her. "Kyle, do you have an idea how much I love your Mimi?" she said around the lump in her throat.

"This much?" Kyle said, spreading out his arms and splashing them with water.

"Even more!" Krista said, her face beaming.

Melanie giggled. "I love this day!" she exclaimed.

"Kyle," Heather yelled at her son from the cliff. "Do you want to try?"

He looked at the cliffs and then at Krista and Melanie.

"Will you go with me, Mimi?"

"I will," said Melanie.

"Will you catch me, Kwista?" he asked her earnestly.

"Yes sir!" she said confidently.

"Okay, Momma. Here I come," he said, swimming toward the rocks.

"I love you, too," Melanie said softly before she swam after Kyle.

Once Kyle took that first leap he had to go several more times. They all took turns swimming and jumping, and laughter filled the air.

Krista found herself floating with Melanie, Julia, and Heidi, watching the others.

"All we need are Courtney and Becca to make this complete," Krista said.

"Maybe we'll come back Saturday while they're here," said Julia.

"Can you believe we were doing this thirty-two years ago, talking about coming out and our careers?" said Heidi.

"Things are much better than they were," said Krista. "I can't help wishing I'd had more courage."

"We all wish that at times in our life, Krissy," said Julia. "I'm thankful for all those that did have it and made things better for us."

"And for them," said Melanie, indicating the younger ones.

"All we need is to turn up the music and sing!" said Heidi.

Later in the day Krista and Julia climbed in the boat for a drink.

"You know, Heidi and I were talking on the way home last night. Reliving your and Melanie's story was hard."

"Yeah it was," Krista agreed.

"But Krissy, you look better today than you have in weeks, months even," commented Julia.

"What?"

"You do!"

Krista exhaled and found Melanie jumping off a cliff holding Mason's hand. Their splash and then laughter sounded better than any song she'd ever sung.

"Melanie says it's our time."

"Why don't you believe her?"

"I want to, Jules. It's just that every other time when we've thought that, something happened."

"Then don't let it. I wish for once you would grab what's yours and hold on to it!" Julia said, exasperated.

"I tried that with Brooke and look what happened."

"You gave your heart to Melanie Zimmer the first time you saw her. Give her the rest of you! This is your family," Julia said, sweeping her arm towards the cliffs where everyone was either swimming, jumping, but all laughing. "This is where you belong. This is where you are supposed to be, where your soul is home!"

"Dang Jules, are you mad at me?"

"No! I get frustrated with you and for you," she explained.

"You probably know this, but I'm Melanie's only client now and she sold her house."

"You know, y'all were always good at talking, but she's showing you, Krista! She's showing you that you are everything. It's time! Look at those people; they are your strength, my friend."

Krista nodded and knew Julia was right.

23

On the way back all the kids got a turn to drive the boat. When they made it back to the dock and had the boats unloaded Krista looked at the kids and said, "I bet they sleep tonight."

Jennifer laughed. "Me too!"

"Let's go to the restaurant and make sandwiches for dinner," Julia suggested.

"Great idea, Jules. We'll meet you there."

Krista took Melanie and the kids back to their cabins to drop off their towels and life jackets. They changed out of their wet clothes and then went back to the restaurant. Everyone made their own sandwich and replayed the day.

"This was the best day I've had in a long time," Krista said, beginning to put the sandwich makings back in the kitchen.

"It's not over yet," Melanie said, pinning Krista with a look.

"Are you going to walk me all the way to my cabin tonight?" Krista asked.

"I am," Melanie said firmly.

Krista winked. "I brought the golf cart. We can ride."

"Are you going to let me stay?"

"You said you wanted to sleep," Krista said, leaning in the doorway.

"Are you tired?" Melanie asked.

"Of course I'm tired. We chased four kids around all day," Krista said, chuckling.

"And you loved every minute of it."

"I did," Krista agreed.

"Hey y'all," Julia said, bringing a tray into the kitchen. "This is everything. We're going home. What a day," she said, sighing.

"Okay Jules. Are you coming out tomorrow?"

"I've got things I need to do at home. I think you can handle things here," she said, winking at them both.

"I'll call you if I need you," Krista teased.

Julia walked over and hugged her friend and said softly, "You have the strength."

"Thanks Jules, I do now."

She gave Mel a hug and then went back into the restaurant.

"What was that?" Melanie asked, her eyes narrowed.

"Julia let me have it this afternoon while you were swimming."

"Oh?"

"She was reminding me where my strength is."

"I see. Do tell?"

"I'm looking at it," Krista said earnestly.

Melanie nodded, walked over and took Krista's hand and pulled her through the doorway. "Julia is one smart woman."

When they got back into the dining room Stephanie said, "We're going back to the cabin for baths, pj's and bedtime books."

"Baths? We've been swimming all day. Why do we need a bath?" said Mason.

"Because there's dirt on those cliffs and in that water. Let's go," said Jennifer.

"I'm riding with Krista and Mimi," said the kids.

"Not this time," said Mimi. "We're going to Krista's."

"I want to go with you," said Kyle.

"Maybe tomorrow," said Krista.

They made their way out to the deck and Krista locked everything up.

"Uh, I'm not sure I should ask this, but do we need to wait up?" said Stephanie shyly.

"Ha ha, very funny," said Melanie.

"See you tomorrow," Krista said, with a hint of pink on her cheeks.

When they got in the golf cart Melanie stared at her for a moment. "That didn't embarrass you, did it?"

"You know how I am," Krista said, giggling and pushing down on the accelerator.

"After all these years?"

"Yes, after all these years," she said, cutting her eyes toward Melanie and then back to the front.

Melanie leaned over and wrapped her arm around Krista and squeezed her close. "Another reason why I love you; you're so fucking adorable."

This made Krista laugh as she weaved the cart through the trees with the lake on her left. She finally pulled up to a smaller cabin nestled between the water and a group of trees that sheltered it from the road.

"Wow," Melanie said, getting out and looking around. "It feels like it's just us and no one else. Listen," she said, spinning around as a smile grew on her face. "It's so quiet."

"Now do you see why I came out here?"

Melanie stopped and looked at Krista with a sad smile. "I'm so sorry, Kris. I'm sorry for everything," she said, tears stinging her eyes.

Krista hurried over and grabbed her hands. "Stop, Mel. It isn't your fault."

"I could apologize to the end of my days and my heart would still be sorry for what it did to you."

"Please stop apologizing," Krista said, cradling Melanie's face in her hands. "We were living, Mel. We did the best we could. Yes, we both got hurt, but neither one of us wanted to hurt the other. I know that. If anything, the situation hurt us."

The corners of Melanie's mouth turned up and she sighed as she grabbed both of Krista's wrists.

"No more apologies," Krista said softly. She gazed into Melanie's eyes intensely.

For a moment Melanie thought Krista might kiss her. "No more apologies," she repeated.

Krista dropped her hands and looked at her watch. "You still have a few hours to convince me to give you another day," she said, walking around to the back of the cabin.

Melanie chuckled as she followed her. "How am I doing so far?"

Krista glanced over at her and raised her eyebrows, but didn't say anything.

Melanie stopped her by grabbing her arm. "Hey," she said softly. "I was serious. I don't want to overwhelm you, Kris. Tell me if you are, please."

"Melanie, I had one of the best days in I don't know when. The only thing missing was Courtney and Becca. Other than that, it's been perfect."

Melanie's smile brightened her entire face. "Then let's keep going. By the way, I can't wait to see them."

"Me too. Come on," Krista said, taking her hand. "I'll show you around."

They walked onto the back patio that looked out over the small cove. "Let's have a beer down by the water. Or would you rather have wine?" Krista asked as she watched Melanie take in the view.

"Beer is fine. It's beautiful here."

While Krista went inside Melanie took a moment to look at the back of the cabin. There was a screened in porch so the cabin could be enjoyed year round. She was standing on a covered patio that a nice breeze was drifting through. There was a table with four chairs and where the patio ended the grass was thick and plush and grew down to a small beach that was just big enough for two people. She could see the water lapping gently up to the sand and even though the sun had set it was light enough to see just how romantic and secluded this little oasis could be.

She didn't hear Krista come back out, but felt her standing close. "Enjoying the view?"

Melanie glanced over at her. "This is quite a little set-up you have here. Is this like the VIP cabin for the really special people?" Melanie asked, taking her beer from Krista.

Krista chuckled. "We've never rented this cabin."

Melanie looked over at her with raised brows.

"It's so far away from everything and it was the last one we renovated. I think I was secretly keeping it to myself. Don't tell Julia," she said, leaning over and bumping her shoulder against Melanie's.

"Your secret is safe with me," Melanie teased.

"That's our business—keeping secrets," Krista reminded her. "Maybe you could work around here if you get bored in retirement."

"Maybe." Melanie shrugged.

"Let's go down to the water. We can just catch the end of the day," Krista said.

There were two lawn chairs sitting on the edge of the grass and they each sat down and ran their feet through the sand.

"Look right through there," Krista said, indicating a space between the trees on the other side of the cove where the sky was turning a dark purple.

"Can you see the sunset from here?"

"It depends on the time of year, but you almost get it now. In September it should be just right."

Melanie gazed over at Krista and reached for her hand. When Krista took it they interlaced their fingers and sat like that for a while, sipping their beer. Since the beginning they'd often sat in a comfortable silence, letting their hearts do the talking.

Melanie set her beer down, dropped Krista's hand and stood up. She had always felt so bold around Krista and that same feeling was coursing through her as she slipped her shirt over her head and let it fall to the ground. She pushed her shorts down and stepped out of them, kicking them on top of her shirt.

"What are you doing?" Krista asked.

Melanie could hear the smile in her voice. With her back to Krista she unhooked her bra and then stepped closer to the water. She looked over her shoulder and said, "This girl I love once took me skinny dipping. I loved it then and wondered if I still would." She slipped her undies off and walked into the water. When she was thigh deep she turned again and said, "Are you going to join me?" Melanie could feel Krista's eyes roaming over her body and any thoughts of wrinkles and aging were gone when she saw the desire in Krista's eyes.

Krista stood and began to take her clothes off.

"You've always made me fearless when it's just us," Melanie said as she watched Krista. It was like she was unwrapping a gift right before her eyes. Krista was still the most beautiful woman her eyes had ever seen and she filled her heart.

Melanie reached her hand out as a naked Krista walked towards her. When she took it they waded deeper until the water reached just above their chests. "Do you remember?" Melanie asked as she stepped in front of Krista.

"Of course I do," Krista said, putting her arms around Melanie's shoulders and pulling her close.

Melanie's breath caught in her throat and her eyes fluttered shut as Krista put her legs around Melanie's hips. She was wrapped around Melanie, pressing her chest to hers. Melanie could feel Krista's heart beating next to hers.

"What have we done?" Krista whispered. "Why have we let phone calls, texts, and FaceTime replace seeing each other? I feel just like I did thirty years ago—when we're together we can do this, but then when we're apart the doubts and hardships overwhelm my thoughts."

"Then let's not be apart," Melanie said. "I'm never leaving you again, Krista."

"Could we do that? Are we both finally over our fears? Are we finally brave enough to really try?" asked Krista.

"I am," Melanie said. "Look in my eyes, Kris. Can you see my heart? Can you see my soul? It's been waiting so long."

"You won't leave?"

"Never again," Melanie said firmly.

Krista crashed her lips into Melanie's and kissed her, sealing this promise they'd made. This kiss was powerful and forceful and then it turned passionate and neither could get close enough. This was a kiss to make up for all those years apart. Melanie could feel her heart pounding and Krista's in rhythm with it. She could taste beer and smell the freshness of the water around them. Their breathing was labored, but this kiss was like their love: never-ending.

A moan escaped from Krista's throat and it was a melody to Melanie's ears. Her nose was trying to discern the familiar scent she inhaled and then she knew as her heart constricted with love. It was the sunshine that somehow always lingered in Krista's hair. She remembered this from their secret summer in 1991 and every time they were together since she'd get just a whiff of what she knew to be Krista's intoxicating aroma. It was a balm to the longing in her heart because she knew Krista was home, they were home.

Breathless, they pulled apart slightly and Krista grinned. "We never did have problems with this part."

Melanie took a breath and said fervently, "Kiss me!"

Krista's grin fell into a seductive look that made Melanie's knees weak and her stomach drop. Good God, this woman could still light a fire in her that was instantly blazing with so much as a look. This time Krista nibbled Melanie's bottom lip and it was her turn to moan. She could feel Krista kiss along her cheek to her ear and nibble there as well.

"Krista," she whispered on a long exhale.

"Mmm," Krista answered as she kissed down her neck and began to bite a little harder along her pulse point. "I remember promising not to leave a mark, but not anymore," Krista said softly. "You have me almost out of control," she breathed.

Melanie began walking them to the shore with Krista still somewhat wrapped around her. She put her arm around her waist and Krista began walking with her.

When they hit the sand they both hurried, now hand in hand, to the back door.

Krista stopped. "Our clothes?"

"Later," Melanie said with an intense look.

Once inside Krista led them towards the bedroom. "I'll show you around later."

"Thanks," Melanie said abruptly.

When they got to the bedroom Melanie pushed Krista down on the bed and crawled on top of her. She was about to kiss her when Krista put her index finger over Melanie's lips.

"Slow down. We have all night."

Melanie softened and with a twinkle in her eyes said, "It's almost midnight."

She smiled, realizing Melanie was referring to last night when she asked for one day at a time. Who was she trying to fool? She could never say no to Melanie Zimmer, not then and not now. But more importantly, she didn't want to.

"I'll give you tomorrow," Krista said as a grin began to grow on her face. She looked up into Melanie's eyes with such love and said, "And the next day, and the next, and the next … you can kiss me now."

Melanie smiled. "How's your heart?"

Krista's eyebrows shot up her forehead and then she chuckled. "I can't believe I'm talking about Julia in the middle of making love with you, but she said I gave you my heart the first time I saw you. My heart is yours; it has always been yours. It's fragile right now, but you said you have the courage and strength for both of us."

"I do, but I want more than your heart, Krista. I want all of you. My soul has longed for the one it loves."

Krista remembered Melanie saying those words that summer and then she felt her entire being open up, letting Melanie inside. She felt all the feelings she'd tamped down for years rise up and then she felt a rush of love whoosh in her body and slam into her heart.

"Take me," she breathed.

24

Melanie could see the love swirling in Krista's eyes and when she said "take me," Melanie thought her heart stopped. She claimed Krista's lips and made love to her with all of her being. Gently she stroked up and down Krista's body to moans of pleasure and encouragement. Her fingers glided over familiar territory that she adored, worshipped, and loved.

She kissed Krista hard, then soft, then sensuously, then wet and they were the best kisses their lips had ever shared. Melanie straddled Krista and entwined the fingers of both their hands and hovered over her, drinking in Krista's beauty. She kissed her neck and then up to trace the inside of her ear. Krista moaned and writhed under her.

"Fuck Mel," she groaned.

"We'll get to that."

"Oh babe. I need you. Now," panted Krista.

Melanie obliged by sucking Krista's nipple into her mouth.

"Yes," whispered Krista. "You are so good at that."

Melanie smiled against Krista's chest while she kissed her way to the other nipple.

"It's because I love you," Melanie said, kissing her way across and down Krista's stomach. "Every part of you. I want to kiss and touch all of you." She took her hands from Krista's and settled between her legs.

She ran her hands along Krista's outer thighs and then rested them on her stomach. When she looked up into Krista's eyes she felt her lovingly run her hand through her hair. Melanie could see the want and the desire, but there was also understanding because Krista knew she was about to drown in perfect pleasure from the person she loved most.

Krista's heady scent hit Melanie with a shot of pleasure and inspiration. She had waited so long to taste Krista again and she was going to thoroughly seek, savor, and stay as long as Krista would let her.

"Mmm. Baby, baby, baby," Krista moaned.

"Tell me, darling," Melanie said as she lapped up Krista's luscious wetness.

"More, Mel. I want all you've got," Krista said then gasped as Melanie sucked her clit into her mouth.

Melanie loved the moans coming from Krista and she felt Krista's hand fist in her hair as she pulled it slightly. Krista's other hand slammed down on the bed when Melanie slipped two fingers inside her.

"Oh yes!" Krista said loudly and began to move her hips to the rhythm Melanie had started.

Melanie ran her tongue around Krista's clit, lapping up more of her and said, "Kris?"

"I need you to kiss me. Now!" Krista said, pulling Melanie's face to hers.

Melanie knew Krista was close, but she wanted to see the moment the orgasm took her. She wanted their eyes to be locked on one another. So she kissed her and lavished her mouth with love as her fingers curled to find Krista's prized spot. She felt her tense and tore her lips away to see Krista's beatific face.

"Look at me baby," she begged Krista.

Krista's eyes flew open and locked on Melanie's.

"I love you," Melanie said with tears in her eyes.

"Oh I love you," Krista answered.

The orgasm hit Krista and Melanie watched as wave after wave washed over. She could feel the power and euphoria pass into her along with Krista's love.

When the ecstasy began to wane she propped on her elbow as she watched Krista's breathing slow; she smoothed a dark brown curl off her forehead beaded with perspiration. When Krista's eyes opened Melanie wanted to dive into those dark blue orbs, never to return.

"Do you know how long it's been since we've been together like this?" Krista asked quietly.

"A long time. Too long," Melanie answered.

"Were you trying to make up for all that time right now?"

Melanie looked away shyly. "Maybe," she mumbled.

Krista tucked her finger under Melanie's chin and guided her face back to hers. "I could feel the love from all that time pour into me from you," she said tenderly.

"I've always loved you, never stopped, you know that," said Melanie. "And I know you never stopped loving me."

"What the fuck is wrong with us!" Krista said, smoothing her hand over Melanie's hair.

Melanie looked at her, suddenly alarmed.

"We wasted so much time. I will not waste another moment being without you. Do you hear me, Mel?" Krista said, raising her voice.

Melanie nodded and relaxed. "I hear you, baby."

"Now lie back so I can rest my head on your chest. I need to hear your heart beating."

Melanie did as instructed. She'd forgotten that this was indeed one of Krista's favorite things. She loved to lay her head on Melanie's chest and listen to her heart beating wildly after making love and oftentimes they fell asleep this way.

"Don't worry, I'm not falling asleep. I just wanted to hear your heart beating again with us in it."

Melanie chuckled. "My heart has always been beating with us in it," she said, running her hand through Krista's curls.

"Yeah, but I couldn't hear it, not like this."

"Oh baby, you can listen anytime you want," Melanie said with a contented sigh.

* * *

Krista closed her eyes and sighed as a smile played across her face. She couldn't believe the woman she had always loved was sleeping peacefully on her chest. In all the nights they had spent together off and on over the years this was the way they usually woke up. One of them would be resting their head on the other's chest, cuddled in as close as they could get.

This was like the proverbial dream come true because for over half of Krista's life she had dreamed of waking up with Melanie, but this time it was real. What hadn't happened all those times before was the knowledge that this time was for good. They were finally on the same page, as the saying went. That wasn't quite right; they had always been on the same page. They always wanted to be together. But it seemed like there was always something in the way, something stopping them.

Not this time. Krista didn't care what she had to do or what happened, she was staying with Melanie from now on. Melanie had promised to never leave her and she didn't break promises. Krista had said more than once since Melanie showed up at Lovers Landing that she always felt strong when they were together and this morning was no different. They had talked and made love into the early morning and she awoke with more clarity and confidence than ever before.

Krista sighed again. She had been happy many times in her life and had woken up like this, in a haze of loved-up bliss. This morning was different in that neither of them had to be anywhere or do anything for the foreseeable future. Melanie was no longer responsible for the business, her kids were healthy and more than capable of taking care of themselves, and her grandkids were exactly where they should be and needed to be.

Krista didn't care if she ever acted, read another script, or even entertained a group at Lovers Landing again. All she wanted to do was be with Melanie. She stopped herself from giggling because she didn't want to wake Melanie, but her thought was that all she wanted to do was stay right here in this bed, in this little cabin, away from whatever tried to keep them apart this time. But then she took a deep breath, took a moment to be grateful and knew in her heart that this time, they were going to make it.

"Mmm, I can feel you smiling," Melanie mumbled against Krista's chest.

Krista chuckled. "Good morning, lover," she said as she ran her hand up and down Melanie's back. This used to be her favorite way to greet Melanie in the mornings all those years ago.

Melanie's head shot up. "I can't believe you said that!" she said, grinning sleepily.

"It's so 1991, isn't it?"

"I love it," Melanie said, kissing her softly. "And I love you."

"I didn't mean to wake you," she said, smoothing her hand over Melanie's hair. "Come on," she said, snuggling her close. "We can sleep a little longer."

"The kids will be looking for us," she said, planting a kiss on Krista's chest.

"I've already texted that they would not be seeing us until later in the afternoon."

Melanie raised her head and propped it on her hand. "Oh you did."

Krista looked into her warm dark eyes and felt like she was melting in chocolate. "I did."

They held one another for a few moments and Melanie said, "What have you been thinking about? I know if you've been awake something is whirling around that beautiful mind of yours."

Krista squeezed Melanie tighter, but didn't say anything.

"Come on, Kris. This is the part we always mess up."

"What?" Krista said.

"Last night and this morning are the parts we're good at, as you said. But holding one another and letting thoughts run through our heads without speaking them is what gets us in trouble. It's how we hurt one another. And I don't want to hurt you again."

Krista closed her eyes for a moment, taking in Melanie's words. "First, I took a moment to be grateful because in two days time you have once again changed my life. There was no way in the world I was going to be with anyone ever again. I'd made up my mind and here I am living a dream come true. Because that's what you always were, Mel. You were a dream that I couldn't quite hold, that I couldn't make a reality. I'm surprised you didn't wake up earlier because I found myself squeezing you tighter to me all night. Then I looked at what you've done as far as giving everything up to come to me and make this happen. I've been trying to think of what in the world could happen to mess this up."

Melanie pushed up on her hands and crawled on top of Krista. "Nothing is going to mess this up, Kris. Do you hear me? Not this time. We belong together," she said decisively.

Krista took Melanie's concerned face in her hands and said, "It's okay. I keep hearing you say that you're never leaving me again."

"That's right." Melanie nodded ardently. "Never."

"I couldn't think of anything, babe. There's nothing that could come between us. Not this time."

Melanie visibly softened. "We're not going to *let* anything come between us. Damnit, we're supposed to be together. I know it in my soul. We gave up thirty years until the time was right for both of us. It's our time, Krissy."

"It's our time." Krista nodded.

Melanie exhaled and shook her head. "Don't scare me like that."

"You asked what I was thinking and I told you."

Melanie leaned down and kissed her. "You did."

Krista rolled Melanie onto her side and they faced one another. "Ask me what I'm thinking now?" she said in a low sexy voice as she caressed Melanie's cheek.

"I can see what you're thinking because your beautiful blue eyes are almost as dark as the midnight sky," Melanie said with a husky tone of her own. She reached up and mirrored Krista's movements.

"I'm not sorry for all we had to go through to get to this moment because now we have one another, finally and completely," Krista said.

"I'm only looking forward," Melanie said.

Krista leaned in closer and touched her lips to Melanie's. "My soul has longed to be with you like this again. I pushed those feelings down because I never believed it would happen. They have always lingered in the background, sometimes whispering other times louder, but still there. Before I turned around and saw you on the dock two nights ago I knew you were near. That's why I was out walking. I was being guided by my soul. When our eyes met my heart stopped, then fluttered and banged against my chest. I knew then that I couldn't let you get away. I needed a little time to still my heart and let your love surround it."

"My heart told me to be patient, but I knew no matter what, I would never leave you again. That's why when you said my name I let that beautiful sound wash over me and then opened my arms because I wanted you to come to me the way you wanted. It took everything I had to let you go after I held you to my chest, but my heart assured me you'd be back. I wanted to profess my love, adoration, and security right then, but I also knew it would be too much. Thank you Julia," she said, looking up. "She told me how you were doing and when I told her I couldn't wait any longer, she was afraid you weren't ready. But she didn't know the power of our hearts."

"I'm not sure we know the power of our hearts," said Krista, bringing their lips together so softly.

"I've been in love with you for such a long time. That's where our power comes from."

"Love me, Melanie," Krista whispered with such longing in her eyes.

"Love me, Krista," Melanie said, barely loud enough for them to hear. She began to trail her hand down Krista's chest and pressed her palm to her breast.

Krista's eyes fluttered closed, basking in the feel of Melanie's hand. No one ever touched her the way Melanie did. She opened her eyes and took her time running her hand down to caress Melanie's breast. She loved it when they made love like this. Sometimes it was hard to stay focused because Melanie could make her lose awareness, but she also wanted to give her the same joy and pleasure.

Staring into one another's eyes, at the same time they inched their hands down until they could rest their hands between the other's legs. As if they were in a synchronized dance, they each raised their leg up giving the other access.

Krista gasped when she felt Melanie's wetness and then couldn't breathe when she felt Melanie's fingers circle her clit. It was a double shot of arousal and passion. The corners of her mouth flickered upward showing Melanie how good she made her feel.

"This is incredible," Krista breathed. "I can't get enough of you." She pushed one finger inside Melanie and watched the gratification shine in her eyes as she added another.

"Oh Kris, yes. Mmm," she moaned. Then she slipped two fingers inside Krista to louder moans of joy.

"Fuck yes, Mel. You know just what I want," she panted. "Come here," she said, leaning over so their lips could meet. "God I love kissing you."

"Kissing has always been your favorite."

"Come on baby, let's go." Krista started to slowly move in and out and waited for Melanie to join in the rhythm. She couldn't decide which was better, being inside Melanie or Melanie being inside her. Right now it didn't matter as they both came closer and closer to the ultimate paradise they sought.

"This is so fucking good," Melanie moaned as she leaned over and kissed Krista.

When their tongues met Krista was almost done. Nothing tasted better than Melanie, but she pulled away so she could gaze into her eyes as they fell together.

"Ready?"

"Mmm, yes," Melanie said, her chest rising and falling to the rhythm of their love.

Krista pushed deeper and curled her fingers and found Melanie's pleasure spot.

"Mmm, Krista!" she yelled. Then she did the same, finding Krista's spot and letting her fingers work their magic.

"Melanie," Krista groaned as they were joined together and came together. Neither of them moved as the waves of pleasure washed over them again and again.

When the orgasm began to wane Melanie smiled at Krista with a knowing look. "That was so good. It amazes me when we do it like that and I love it so much."

"I love *you* so much," Krista said, her voice thick with emotion.

"And I love you," Melanie answered. "I hope you like hearing that because I'm saying it all the time now."

"The way my name slides off your lips is almost as good as hearing 'I love you,'" Krista said.

"I know!" Melanie exclaimed. "When you say my name it makes my heart flutter and fill with joy."

"Good God, Mel," Krista said. "Could we have gotten sappier with age?"

"Who cares!"

They both laughed and nestled next to one another, quickly falling into a much needed nap.

25

"Thanks again for getting my clothes from the sand," Melanie said, taking a bite of an apple slice. "Or did I thank you already."

The smile on Krista's face broadened. "You thanked me, but maybe you'll need to again later."

Melanie chuckled. "I'd be happy to."

"Do you think we could stay here the rest of the day?" Krista leaned over and kissed her on the lips. "I kind of like keeping you to myself."

After their nap both their stomachs were empty and protesting loudly. Krista had thrown together some fruit, cheese, and crackers for an impromptu picnic on the back patio.

"I actually have plans for us later."

"Oh?" Krista asked, her face full of surprise.

"I think this is the night the kids were going to the drive-in."

"They really are recreating that summer. Do you want to go to the drive-in?"

"No. I hoped I could get you all to myself."

Krista smiled. "And what were you going to do with me?"

"It's kind of a surprise, but we will need the boat."

"Are you going to take me skinny dipping in the middle of the lake?"

Melanie chuckled. "No, but we can do that when we get back." She sat up in her chair and leaned closer to Krista. "You do remember that I hadn't been skinny dipping until that summer with you, right?"

"I do remember that."

"The only times I've been skinny dipping are with you," she said, resting her chin in her hand. "I know you can't say the same, but I wanted you to know that."

Krista had a hint of a smirk on her face and leaned toward Melanie and put her chin in her hand. "For your information, since that night we first skinny dipped, I have not been skinny dipping with anyone but you. I like swimming naked, but only with you."

Melanie's face brightened. "I'm not sure we do much swimming, do we?"

Krista shrugged. "Does it matter?"

A rich laugh bubbled up from Melanie's chest. "Not at all. As long as we're together I'm finding that not much else does matter."

Krista leaned a little closer, but stopped before their lips touched and sighed. "I love you so much," she said with more contentment than she'd ever felt.

"I love you, too," Melanie replied, closing the minute distance between their lips.

When their lips parted, Krista said, "Let's go check in with the kids and get your stuff."

Melanie raised her eyebrows. "My stuff? Are you giving me another day?" she teased.

"If you'll remember I gave you all my days last night."

"I'll never forget it," Melanie said, a little breathless.

Krista narrowed her eyes. "Is the memory of last night playing through your mind right now?"

Melanie quirked an eyebrow. "It certainly is."

Krista captured Melanie's lips and kissed her firmly. When she deepened the kiss Melanie slid her hand behind Krista's neck, holding their lips together. This kiss was both familiar and new; it signaled what they both wanted next while knowing their time together now was never-ending.

Melanie eased her hold and leaned back slightly. "I could devour you right now."

Krista's eyes burned into Melanie's and then both of their phones pinged.

They both froze and then Krista smiled. "Later?"

"Oh yeah," Melanie said, nodding.

They both got the same text from Stephanie: *Are we going to see you today?*

"Can you hear the sarcasm in her voice?" asked Krista, laughing.

Melanie giggled. "I can."

"You'd think since they want us together so badly they'd leave us alone," Krista said, staring at her phone.

"When have they ever left us alone?"

Krista looked up at Melanie and chuckled. "That's true. Some nights I didn't think they'd ever go to bed!"

Melanie met her eyes with a smile and chuckled with her. "I know!"

As she texted, Krista said, "Let's get this over with. We'll see them, get your stuff and let them know they are on their own for the evening."

"Perfect."

They cleared the table and drove over to the cabins where their family waited. When they walked up to the back porch Jennifer eyed her mother up and down.

"I guess you two had a nice night."

Melanie grinned at Krista and then smirked at Jennifer. "Is it obvious?"

"Sort of, since you aren't wearing the clothes you left in," she said sarcastically with a smirk.

"How do you know? You haven't seen all my clothes, Jenny," Melanie said defiantly.

Jennifer chuckled. "Well Mom, that's true. I may not have seen *all* your clothes, but I'm pretty sure that isn't your T-shirt."

Melanie looked over at Krista who was looking at her feet and trying not to laugh. Then she looked at her shirt and noticed it was an alumni shirt from Krista's college. "You could help me out?" she said to Krista.

She walked over and took Melanie's face in her hands and kissed her soundly. A grin was plastered on her face. "Jenny, I am madly in love with your momma. She wears my clothes, I wear her clothes, and sometimes we don't wear clothes," she said, her eyes never leaving Melanie's. She looked over at Jenny and added, "We are here now to get her clothes."

Melanie looked at her with the most beautiful smile and said, "And I love you, too."

Before Jennifer could say anything the back door swung open and Kyle came bounding out. "Mimi!" he said, wrapping his arms around both her legs. "Where have you been? You didn't sleep in your room last night."

Melanie ruffled his hair. "I stayed with Krista last night."

"You did? Is Krista going to stay with us tonight?"

"No, I'm going to stay with her again."

He looked up at her and then at Krista. "Can I stay with you tonight?"

Krista grinned at Melanie and then looked down at Kyle. "You can, but I think tonight you're going to the movies. Let's do it another night. Would that be okay?"

"Yep. I forgot we were going to the movies," he said, jumping up and down.

"Do you want to help me pack my stuff?" Melanie asked, holding out her hand.

"Sure," he said, taking Melanie's hand. They walked inside and Krista looked over at Jennifer.

"So, you and my mom, huh," Jennifer said, feigning seriousness.

Krista could see the corners of her mouth begin to turn up and before she could say anything Stephanie came flying out of the house. She threw her arms around Krista, almost knocking her down.

"Whoa! What a greeting," Krista said, holding on so they both wouldn't fall.

"Do you have any idea how long we've wanted to call you Mom?" Stephanie said earnestly.

"Wait, what?"

"Let's sit," Jennifer said, indicating the chaise lounge.

Krista sat between the girls on the lounge section of the chair. She chuckled then looked at the girls. "On the day of our very first date, I came by to see your mom at lunch. She was sitting in a chaise lounge reading a book. This isn't the same one." Krista chuckled. "But I've always had one on this back porch."

"Where were we?"

"It was the first weekend you went to see your dad. I came over that Friday night."

"And?"

Krista grinned. "I was very nervous, but we both managed to find the courage to ask a few pointed questions and then planned to go out the next night. We actually went to the cliffs with Julia and Heidi first and then came here." Krista tilted her head, her brow furrowed in thought. "That wouldn't be much of a first date now, but we had to be careful." She shrugged.

Krista looked at them and said, "Now what's this about calling me mom?"

"I remember a night or two before we were leaving to go back home, Jenn and I were in bed." Stephanie stopped and laughed. "For two kids that didn't want to come here we sure were sad we had to go back home."

Jennifer chuckled. "Yeah we were. I said to Steph that it would be cool if you were our mom too."

Krista exhaled. "I can't tell you how many times I've thought of you both as my girls." She put an arm around each of them and pulled them close.

Melanie along with Heather and Kyle came out the back door.

"If this doesn't make a mom happy," Melanie said.

"Family picture," Heather said, taking her phone out of her pocket.

"Come on," Krista said, patting her lap.

"If I remember it was the other way around," Melanie said.

Krista laughed. "You're right." She got up and let Melanie sit and then she sat in her lap with her arms around both the girls. They smiled at Heather while Kyle said, "Say cheese!"

"I love it!" Jennifer said, jumping up. "Our first family photo."

"What? We have lots of pictures of us together," Melanie said with her arms around Krista.

"Not like this. Now we know the truth and you two can be honest about your feelings for one another," explained Stephanie.

"I'll text it to you," Heather said happily.

"Where is everybody?" Krista asked, getting off Melanie's lap.

"The boys are over making sure they have all their fishing stuff. They want to go tomorrow so I told them if they needed something we could get it while we're in town tonight."

"Oh. I have plenty of fishing stuff too if they need anything," Krista said.

"You do?" asked Melanie.

"You'd be surprised how many of our guests want to fish. I think it's being in nature and out of the city. Do y'all remember when we went fishing?"

"I do," said Stephanie.

"Me too," added Jennifer.

"Your mom expected me to bait your hooks and take the fish off because I work here," Krista said, giving Melanie a look.

"You didn't like doing that?" said Jennifer.

"No! I still don't like it," said Krista.

"Me neither!" stated Stephanie looking at Heather.

"I hear you," said Heather.

They all laughed then Jennifer said to Krista, "I remember you taking us to the drive-in and letting us sit in front. I don't need to know what you were doing in the backseat with my mother," she said, making a face. "But I thought it was really cool of you to take us to the movies."

"I loved you," Krista said sweetly. "And still do. For your information I was holding your mom's hand in the backseat, that's all."

"I'd better go get those boys ready and Kyle you'd better go see if your sister is ready to go," Jennifer said.

"I think we're going to do it, just like we did thirty years ago, and hit McDonald's first." Stephanie grinned.

"Have fun," Melanie said, hugging both her daughters and Heather.

"Y'all too," said Stephanie suggestively.

"Oh we will," Krista said, walking off wiggling her hips and then bumping Melanie with her butt.

"Look at them," Heather said. "I've got the coolest mother-in-laws... or is it mothers-in-law?"

"Moms!" said Stephanie, kissing her on the cheek.

26

"It was nice making dinner together. We haven't done that in a long time," said Krista, putting the leftovers away.

"Gosh, I can't even remember the last time we did this," Melanie said, looking at Krista as she closed the dishwasher door.

"So what's next, Miss Romance?" Krista asked, grabbing Melanie around the waist and kissing her cheek.

"Are you excited?" Melanie asked, putting her arms around Krista's shoulders.

"You know I am. I've been ready since we got back with your stuff."

"Is that why you were so helpful putting my clothes away?" Melanie grinned.

Krista's face turned serious. "It brought me such joy to put your clothes away. It means you're staying."

"I am," Melanie whispered, kissing her softly. "We'd better go before we get sidetracked. I can't seem to keep my hands off you."

Krista smiled, resting her forehead on Melanie's. "I know," she exhaled.

Melanie kissed her quickly on the lips and dropped her arms.

"Let me get a couple of things and I'll be ready. I'll meet you at the golf cart."

"I can help," Krista said.

"No, go! It's a surprise," Melanie said, shooing her out of the house. Once Krista was gone, Melanie took a bottle of wine and a container out of the fridge and put them in a backpack along with a couple of plastic glasses and a few snacks. There was already a blanket in the bag she'd packed earlier. She took a deep breath and joined Krista at the golf cart.

"Move over, babe," Melanie said, sitting the bag in the back.

Krista raised her eyebrows as she slid over to the other side of the front seat. "Hmm, I love it when you're pushy."

Melanie giggled, then in a sexy voice said, "I know you do."

Krista looked at her with such love and put her arm on the back of the seat. "Take me away, darling."

Melanie smiled over at her and hit the accelerator. "I did have help planning and getting things together for this, so we'll thank Julia tomorrow."

"What exactly did she help you with?"

"Well, I wanted to take you somewhere on the lake where you don't always go, so Julia gave me a couple of suggestions."

Krista rubbed across Melanie's shoulders as the dock came into sight. "You know, it doesn't matter where we go as long as I'm with you."

Melanie looked over at her as she stopped the golf cart. "I know that, but I want to do something special for you just like you were always doing for me."

Krista leaned over and took Melanie's chin in her hand and kissed her. "You made me want to."

"You *make* me want to," Melanie parroted, widening her eyes. They laughed and walked up to the dock hand in hand.

Once in the boat Melanie looked at Krista and said, "Do you trust me to drive?"

"Of course I do," she said, untying the boat and pushing them away from the dock. She sat down in the passenger seat as Melanie steered them out of the cove and toward the main part of the lake.

They headed in the direction of the cliffs and Krista leaned over and yelled over the wind and sound of the motor. "Are you taking me to the cliffs?"

Melanie shook her head and once they got near the cliffs she guided them around to the backside where they usually swam.

"Are we swimming?" Krista asked, since the noise had quieted.

"Nope," Melanie said. She guided them to the far side of the cove and just as Julia had explained, she saw a slight break in the trees. The shore was sandy so she pointed the nose of the boat for the trees and began to reduce their speed. She cut the engine and let them glide until they softly nudged the sand and the boat came to a stop.

"Nice job," said Krista, impressed.

"Thanks," Melanie said, a lilt of pride in her voice. She grabbed the bag and stepped over the side into the water. Then she turned to Krista and offered her hand.

Krista took it and stepped over the side. Once she was in the water she stumbled and Melanie easily caught her. "I've got you."

"Don't ever let me go," Krista said, holding on.

"Never again," Melanie promised.

With just a few steps they made it to the beach. They shook the water from their feet and put their sandals back on.

"Do you know where we're going?"

"I haven't been up here since I was a kid. My dad used to bring me." Krista grinned.

"Oh good. Come on, babe," Melanie said, reaching for Krista's hand.

They made their way into the trees and up the trail.

"It feels like we're all by ourselves in here," Melanie said, referring to the shade and the canopy of the trees.

"I know. It's like we stepped into another world."

They continued hiking as the trail snaked up the hill and then they walked through the trees to a clearing. The lake glistened a beautiful blue below them with the sun just above the horizon.

"Look at this!" Krista gasped.

Melanie quickly opened the bag and spread out a blanket. "I've got you a front row seat to this evening's spectacular sunset ordered just for you, my love," she said, patting the blanket next to her.

Krista plopped down beside her with such delight on her face.

"Wow," Melanie said, a little breathless.

"What?" Krista said, still smiling.

"You're beautiful. That's what," Melanie said, kissing her.

"Thank you," Krista said shyly.

Melanie took out the wine and the glasses. "You pour," she instructed Krista while she took out the other container and crackers.

"What's in there?" Krista asked as she poured.

"You'll see," Melanie said.

Krista handed her a glass and Melanie said, "Thank you for telling our story to the girls and for giving me another chance."

"I can't say no to you. You know that," Krista said, clinking her plastic glass to Melanie's. They took a drink and then Krista said, "Here's to finally living the life we always wanted. Because I know in my heart you wanted this as much as I did. I'm sorry it took us so long to get here, but none of that matters now because we *are* here."

"I love you, Kris."

"I love you too, Mel. I never stopped loving you."

"I know that," she said sweetly. "Close your eyes," she said.

"What?"

"I have a surprise, close your eyes."

Krista did as Melanie instructed and waited.

Melanie spread what was in the container on a cracker and told Krista, "Okay, now open your mouth."

"I'm trusting you," Krista said cautiously.

"I won't let you down, now open."

Krista did and took a small bite. She kept her eyes closed as she chewed and the joy grew on her face. She popped her eyes open. "Is that pimento cheese?"

"It is," Melanie said, grinning.

"Aw babe, I haven't had this in so long." She opened her mouth for Melanie to feed her the rest of the cracker. "Whenever I have pimento cheese I think of my mom and you," she said, taking another cracker from Melanie.

They took turns spreading the mixture on crackers and feeding one another. Krista happily sighed and they watched the sun begin its descent.

"You know, the last three months all I did was think about what led up to that day with Brooke."

Melanie patiently waited.

"I thought back to us and then to my relationship with Tara. I loved her, but I knew deep down she'd leave. I wasn't ready to come out and I still thought that someday you and I could be together. We were always in the back of my mind. It had been years since I'd been with anyone when we opened this place. Have I thanked you lately for making me all this money so I could buy this place?"

"Yes you have," Melanie chuckled.

Krista looked at her. "You were right, I was lonely when Brooke came along. Here's what I think happened. I have always wanted what Julia and Heidi have. And in my mind that was with you. When Tara left and you and I didn't work out again, I focused on work and then this place. I think with Brooke I found someone who had been hiding and I knew I could help her because I'd done the same thing for so long. I talked myself into thinking I wanted to marry her because that would end this crazy notion in my head that you were the one. If I was married to someone else then that voice would finally go away and I could sort of have what Julia and Heidi have. How fucked up is that!"

"Babe, I get it. I truly believe our hearts, souls, whatever you want to call it, became one that summer. I guess they married whether the rest of us were ready or not. I know it sounds strange, but here's what I do know. We love each other and we belong together. No matter what has happened or what we've done to keep us apart it's not as strong as our love for one another. We're together now. And we're living our forever."

Krista loved that woman so much. Everything had become crystal clear to her since she saw Melanie on the dock that night. She could breathe again, her heart was happy and she was living again. Leaning toward Melanie, she caressed the side of her face and brought their lips together softly. Those were the lips she was meant to be kissing. These lips fit perfectly with hers and she could feel the happiness in her heart that only they could bring.

Melanie pulled away slightly. "We're missing this sunset that I ordered especially for you."

Krista smiled against Melanie's lips. "We're not missing a thing," she said, kissing her again.

When they looked again the sun had fallen between two mountains just as Julia had described it to Melanie.

"Look at that!" Krista exclaimed. "It looks like it's falling into the water. How beautiful."

"The colors!" Melanie said, awed.

With arms around each other, they watched as the sun touched the water and then sank, but not before bathing the sky in the brightest hues of yellow, orange, red, and purple.

When it began to get dark they put the wine, glasses, pimento cheese and crackers back in the backpack. They were kneeling on the blanket when Melanie stopped and said, "Do you want to get married?"

Krista thought for a moment. "Do you?"

"I want to do what you want to do. If you want to be married then we'll do it."

"I think you're right. Our hearts have been married since the summer of 1991. Let's pick a date and we'll start celebrating that as our anniversary."

Melanie sat back and laughed. "That's a great idea! June fourth."

"What?"

"That's the day. Trust me, I know. I remember."

"That was the day when–"

"That was the day our souls came together. I remember it like yesterday and I knew you felt it too because I could see it in your eyes. It scared you."

"It did, but I knew you were mine and I'd just given myself to you."

"Everything changed that night."

Krista smiled at her with such love. "Everything changed." She leaned over and gave her a quick kiss. "Come on, we'd better get down while we can still see."

They made it into the boat and started towards Lovers Landing. The trip back was slower and the breeze a little cooler. They were content to hold hands, exchange smiles and received an extra treat watching the moon come up and light their way.

Krista tied the boat to the dock and held her hand out for Melanie to get out of the boat.

"Talk about romance. Babe, you gave me a brilliant sunset followed by a ride home by moonlight," Krista said.

"Let's go home and watch the stars," Melanie replied. She stopped and turned to Krista. "Speaking of home…"

"Do you want to make the cabin our home?"

"I don't know. It just came out," Melanie explained.

"You don't want to move back into our original cabin once the girls leave?"

"I kind of like the little secluded one we're in now. How about you?"

"You know what I'm going to say."

Melanie chuckled. "Wherever I am is where you want to be."

"Exactly."

"Let's talk about it later. Right now I want to howl at the moon, look at a few stars and then you never know what might happen," Melanie said, wiggling her eyebrows.

"I know what I hope happens," Krista said, chuckling.

27

"I could get used to lazing around in bed with you all morning," Krista said, cuddling Melanie closer.

"We didn't get to do that much did we?" she replied. "No reason we can't now."

"I was thinking that it would be fun to have a big party and announce to the world our intentions," Krista said, putting her hands to her mouth like a megaphone. "You know how nosy our family is."

"And what are your intentions?" Melanie giggled.

"I'm doing everything I want to do right here," Krista said, kissing Melanie softly. "We can make it Stephanie's birthday party too, or did y'all just use that as an excuse to come here?"

"Kind of, but we can do one big party for all of it." Melanie's eyes widened and she asked, "Will you dance with me?"

"I will."

"God, I loved dancing with you," Melanie said, closing her eyes.

"We can dance and sing and do whatever you want!" Krista said.

Melanie gasped excitedly. "Will you sing to me?"

Krista couldn't stop the smile on her face. "I might," she said and then shook her head. "Oh, who am I kidding. Of course I'll sing to you if that's what you want."

"Thank you," Melanie said, kissing her.

"But I might want something in return," she said, raising her eyebrows.

"You don't have to sing to me for that," Melanie said, nuzzling and kissing her neck.

"Mmm," Krista moaned. "What do you want to do next?"

"Well..." Melanie giggled, nipping her neck. Then she sat up and looked in Krista's eyes. "I don't have to be anywhere or do anything. I can do everything from my phone or computer. I do have to close on the house and move my things somewhere. What do you want to do next?"

Krista felt a wave of nostalgia roll through her. "This is so much better," she mumbled.

"What is?"

Krista sighed. "Do you remember when we would try to plan the next time we could be together?"

"Yes." Melanie nodded. "This time is so much better because we know it's going to happen. Secrets or work can't get in the way this time."

"Nope."

"What do you have coming up? You know I'm coming with you wherever you have to go."

Krista furrowed her brow and stared at Melanie. "Honestly, I think I'm done," she said, her face softening.

"What do you mean?" Melanie asked, quirking an eyebrow.

"I don't have any projects scheduled that I have parts in. I read over a few scripts that might be good projects for Ten Queens, but someone else can do that. The next group to come to Lovers Landing is a week out. There is a production meeting here next week. I think this is the perfect time to back away from all that and jump into the middle of this life I've always wanted to live with you."

"Seriously? I don't mean for you to quit working," said Melanie.

"I know that, but what if I want to? You always told me you'd make me enough money to quit when I wanted to. That time is now."

"Are they going to be mad at you? I mean, you haven't been up and running that long."

"I don't care if they are mad, but I wouldn't leave them if they weren't in capable hands. I have the best assistant."

"Presley." Melanie nodded. "We've spoken on the phone several times in the last few years."

"I forgot about that," Krista said, smiling.

"What's that smile about?"

"I was remembering Presley giving me a message from you once."

When Krista didn't continue Melanie said, "And?"

"She noticed my smile when I read the message and commented that no one makes my eyes light up the way your name did."

"I knew she was a smart woman," Melanie said, winking.

"How about you and I go to LA and do the things we wanted to but couldn't because of my fear?" Krista asked.

"It wasn't just your fear. Stop saying it like you did something wrong. Remember, we're looking forward."

Krista nodded and felt such gratitude that they were there together.

"That's a good start. Where do you want to live? We need a home base," said Melanie.

"I don't want to be far from the kids," Krista stated. "I want to go to all their games, performances, and anything else they do. You know, like the proud grandmother. And I want to spend time with the girls. Is all of this okay with you?"

"Yes," Melanie said and happily sighed. "This sounds perfect."

Krista looked around and then at Melanie. "I don't see how we can leave the lake. This is the place we first fell in love and this is the place that brought us together again. It's like our magical home."

"I'm fine staying right here. We'll be close to Julia and Heidi, too. I do have one request," Melanie said shyly.

"What's that?"

"I'd like to help you with a group that comes to Lovers Landing."

Krista smiled. "You know, I made Lovers Landing just like our summer. Our guests do the same things we did. I guess deep down I kept thinking maybe we'd have a different ending if I kept recreating our summer." Krista paused. "That just now occurred to me. Fuck!"

"It's okay, babe. It looks like it worked. Here we are," Melanie said, taking Krista's face in her hands.

"I've been absent from my duties here for the last three months. Becca has been running things. Courtney will be here the rest of the summer to help. Julia takes care of the business end of things, but we can help with the next group," Krista said with a huge smile on her face. "This will be so much fun!"

"Who would have thought my retirement job would be entertaining Hollywood lesbians!" she squealed.

"I know a Hollywood lesbian you can entertain right now," Krista said, wiggling her eyebrows.

Melanie laughed and kissed Krista squarely on the lips. "Come on babe, we've got a party to plan."

***

Jennifer was standing on the deck behind the restaurant watching Krista and Melanie playing with the kids in the water. The boys were trying to paddle board, but Krista kept wiggling their boards and knocking them off. The laughter that drifted up to her was like music. Ava and Kyle were helping their cousins without much success.

She was deep in thought when she felt someone standing next to her. Startled, not recognizing the woman, she said, "Who are you?"

The woman laughed. "I'm Courtney, Julia and Heidi's daughter. Krista is my–" she paused. "She's my godmother, aunt; she's everything wrapped into one."

Jennifer smiled. "Yeah, I get it. She's my other mom."

Courtney looked her up and down.

Jennifer stared back at Courtney and said, "What's that look about?"

"Don't hurt her; she's been through a lot," Courtney warned.

"Calm down. Look at her. Believe me, she's where she's supposed to be. They should've been together years ago."

"I remember my mom talking about your mom and Aunt Krissy talking about Steph and Jenn," Courtney said, watching Krista.

"I'm Jennifer," she said, holding out her hand. "Sorry I was abrupt earlier."

Courtney took her hand. "No worries. I didn't mean to sneak up on you." She let her hand go and added, "You were kind of in your own little world."

"Yeah, just thinking about a conversation I had with Krista," she said.

Courtney chuckled. "Krista is always teaching us 'life lessons,' as she likes to call them."

"Oh really?"

"I have to admit, she's usually spot on." Courtney laughed as Krista tipped Preston off his paddle board.

About that time Krista noticed Courtney and waved. Courtney said to Jennifer, "She loves kids and so do I." She waved back as Krista yelled at her and started to walk out of the water.

"Here she comes. It was nice to meet you," Courtney said as she hurried toward Krista.

"Courtney! What a surprise!" Krista said, wrapping her in a hug.

"I decided to come a day early to check on my favorite aunt," Courtney said, hugging her tightly.

"Aww," Krista said, cupping the side of her face. "Mel, come here!" she yelled over her shoulder.

"A quick life lesson, sweetie. Never give up," Krista said to Courtney.

Melanie walked up to them with a smile on her face. "Oh my gosh, this can't be Courtney."

"It is!" Krista said. "Courtney, this is Melanie. You may remember us talking about her. Anyway," Krista said, putting her arm around Melanie, "she's my happily-ever-after."

Melanie looked over at Krista and then at Courtney. "You were just a kid the last time I saw you."

Courtney stuck out her hand. "It's nice to see you again."

Melanie took her hand and said, "I know how protective you are of Krista. I promise all I want to do is make her happy."

They held one another's gaze and then Courtney smiled. "I can tell that's what you're doing." Courtney turned to Krista. "You look incredible, Aunt Krissy!"

She smiled over at Melanie. "Courtney was my protector for a few days after that wedding fiasco. She has checked in on me regularly since then. I didn't look so great the last time she saw me." Krista grinned, wrinkling her nose.

"I'm going to do all I can to keep that smile on her face, Courtney," Melanie said earnestly.

Courtney smiled. "I've heard all about you, Melanie, and from what I see, I know you will."

Krista and Melanie looked at one another. "Oh you have?" said Krista. "I'm thinking your moms put in a good word."

"And your daughter," Courtney said, looking at them both.

Krista's brow furrowed and then she looked past Courtney and saw Jennifer standing on the deck. She smiled. "You met Jennifer?"

"I did. She assured me that you're where you're supposed to be."

Melanie studied Courtney and said, "She wasn't rude was she?"

"I'm getting the idea that we're both protective of you, Aunt Krissy," said Courtney.

"I'm happy to report that none of you have to protect me any longer." She put her arm back around Melanie. "I have my love right here and that's all I need."

Melanie saw Julia walk out of the restaurant and come towards them. "Have you said hello to your mom yet?" she asked Courtney.

"No, I saw y'all first."

"Is that my baby?" Julia called, walking up to them.

Courtney rolled her eyes and turned to hug her mom. "Hi Mama, I saw Krista and wanted to check on her. I was on my way in to see you."

"I'm so glad you're here. You can help me with this party."

"I'd love to. Are we doing karaoke?"

"Maybe," said Krista. "We're dancing, right Jules?"

"That's right. Hey, I ran into Lauren today in town and invited her to the party," said Julia.

"Oh good. Lauren is a friend of ours from high school. She sold us this place," Krista explained.

"Talk about protective," said Courtney. "She's had a crush on Aunt Krissy for a long time."

"That's not true! Y'all have got to stop saying that," Krista grumbled.

"What?" said Melanie, her curiosity obviously piqued.

"She's a very good friend and Jules likes to tease me about her. And this one," she said, throwing her arm around Courtney's neck, "likes to join in."

"Say what you want," said Courtney. "I'm telling you, Melanie—be prepared because she's going to have questions, especially after Brooke."

Krista groaned. "It'll be fine. She knows how I feel about Melanie."

"She does?" asked Julia.

"She came by not long after Brooke left and we got to talking. She knows Melanie is my first love and the one I always wanted to be with. She's a good listener."

"Then I can't wait to meet her." Melanie squeezed Krista's arm.

"Let's go inside. These kids are going to turn into fish if they're in the water much longer. Courtney can meet everyone else," said Krista, smiling at her. "I'm really glad you're here."

28

Krista stopped and happily exhaled. *It doesn't get any better than this.* Melanie was sitting in one of the two old adirondack chairs that overlooked the beach. The kids were playing in the water and their laughter brought the most beautiful smile to Melanie's face.

She walked over and leaned down, bringing their lips together. "Mmm, I could do this all day," Krista said, beginning to stand back up.

Melanie grabbed her around the neck. "Wait, I need one more."

Krista smiled against her lips and kissed her softly. "I've always got a kiss for you."

"Hey, there are kids on this beach," Jennifer catcalled from the water.

Krista waved her off and sat in the chair next to Melanie. "Becca assures me everything is ready for the party tonight. Our chef and bartender are here doing their thing and Steph and Heather are getting things set up for the kids. I tried to tell her this was her party too, but she wasn't having any of it. I think our oldest may not be embracing the idea of turning forty just yet."

"I don't think anyone is happier that we're together than she is.

That's why she's playing down her birthday. Your idea to have video games and movies in the restaurant while we dance in the bar is genius."

"I figured we would all be going in and out of both places and the kids won't get bored," said Krista.

"Have you noticed Jennifer and Courtney spending a lot of time together since she got here?" Melanie asked as she watched them both playing with the kids in the water.

"Courtney loves kids, that's why she became a teacher." Krista watched them for a minute and said, "Maybe something is happening there. Do you remember Jennifer ever being interested in women?"

"No, but they didn't have a clue I was in love with you all these years and she doesn't tell me everything."

"They knew. Anyway, we were talking yesterday about relationships and protecting your heart after you've been hurt. I just told her she had to be open because she has too much love to give and she'd know when the right person comes along for her and for the boys."

Melanie looked over at her. "Another one of your life lessons." Then she added, "Do you really think they knew?"

"Yes, they just couldn't quite figure it out. I think they always wondered."

"Wondered what?" Heather asked, walking up behind them.

"Did Stephanie ever think I was in love with Krista?"

"Nope. I told her you were, but she wouldn't believe me. She said y'all were best friends," Heather said, making air quotes with her fingers. "But Jennifer thought there was something between you because of the way you held one another instead of hugging like most people."

"We were so fucking desperate for each other!" Krista exclaimed. "I couldn't let go."

Melanie laughed. "Good God, I'm glad that's over. I thought my heart was going to break in two."

Krista looked over at her with a sympathetic look. "I know!"

Melanie got up and stood in front of Krista and held out her hands. "Come on, let's go get ready for the party and I'll show you how my heart is now," she said, wiggling her eyebrows.

"This is your party," Heather reminded them. "Don't be late." She chuckled.

"We won't," Krista said, taking Melanie's hands and kissing her.

* * *

The music was playing, everyone had a drink and the chef had plenty of food on the buffet table. When the song they were dancing to ended Krista said, "Let's go check on the kids."

They walked from the bar into the restaurant and saw Courtney challenging Mason in a video game. Jennifer was cheering them on while Ava and Preston were watching something on TV. When Kyle saw them walk in he ran over and said, "Kwista, will you be my Lita?"

"What?" Krista asked, looking from him to Melanie.

She shrugged and shook her head when Heather spoke up from behind.

"Why don't you explain, honey," Heather said, smiling down at her son.

"Preston and Mason have two grandmas and so does Courtney. I only have one. Momma said that she used to have an abuelita, but she died. That's the word for grandma in Spanish," he said, proud of himself. "Since I'm half Latino and I have a Mimi, will you be my abuelita?"

Tears welled up in Krista's eyes as she kneeled down in front of Kyle. "I'd love to be your abuelita."

"Why are you crying?" Kyle asked, tilting his head with bewilderment.

"Because you make me so happy," she said, her voice shaky.

He threw his arms around her neck and squeezed. "I love you, Lita!" Then he let go and ran over to Courtney and Mason and said, "I have two grandmas now too, Courtney."

"Good for you, Kyle. Do you want to help me?" she asked, smiling over at Krista. He climbed in her lap and giggled.

Krista looked at Heather and shook her head.

"He's been asking a lot of questions about families. There are several Latino kids in his class and they have abuelos and abuelas. He doesn't want to miss out on anything," Heather said, chuckling.

"Your parents are missing out," said Melanie.

"I can't believe they won't accept you and Stephanie and their own grandkids," added Krista.

"Hey, it's their loss."

"And my gain!" said Krista, with a new round of tears in her eyes. "I can't believe all this," she said, sniffling.

Melanie wrapped her in her arms. "Oh baby, it's okay."

"I know, Mel. I'm just so happy and my heart is so full it may burst," she said, holding on tight.

"He's been thinking about this since we got here, asking all sorts of questions before he goes to sleep. After talking to his cousins and Jenny this afternoon he asked me if you could be his Lita. I told him to ask you." Heather smiled at Krista.

"We have a family, babe," Krista said to Melanie, her voice full of emotion.

"*We* do," Melanie said proudly and then kissed Krista on the lips.

"The kids also asked me why Mimi and Krista are kissing so much," Heather teased.

"No they didn't," Krista gasped.

"Yes they did, Ask Steph," Heather said as she walked up and put her arm around her wife.

Krista narrowed her eyes. "Did the kids ask you why Mel and I kiss so much?"

"They sure did." Stephanie chuckled.

"What did you tell them?"

"I said y'all kiss because you love each other, just like Momma and I do," Stephanie answered, grinning at Heather and kissing her.

Krista took a shaky deep breath and let it out. "These kids!"

Heather looked at Stephanie and said, "Kyle asked her."

"Aw, that's my boy, making his Lita cry. You did say yes, right?" Stephanie asked.

"Well duh! Of course I did." Krista laughed. "Call me grateful."

"We all are," agreed Heather. "Come on, let's dance. This is supposed to be your party!"

Krista and Melanie walked back into the bar and found Julia and Heidi welcoming Lauren.

"Hey," Krista said, walking up, holding Melanie's hand. "I'm so glad you're here." She turned to Melanie. "Mel, I'd like you to meet my good friend, Lauren Nichols."

Lauren held out her hand and smiled. "I've heard so much about you, Melanie, and I'm so happy to finally meet the girl that Krista fell for that summer so long ago. It'd make a great romance novel or better yet a movie!"

Melanie laughed and grinned. "It's nice to meet you, Lauren."

"I'm sure Julia has told you that I had a huge crush on Krista," Lauren said, giving Julia a look.

Julia's mouth fell open and Krista guffawed.

"I may have had a crush back when we were in high school, but good lord I wouldn't have known what to do with it. Were there any gay people that we knew of in our class?" she asked, looking between Krista and Julia.

"Julia and I wouldn't know. We were almost too afraid to confide in one another."

"Anyway, Krista and I are friends. I know I can talk to her about anything and she won't judge," Lauren said matter-of-factly.

"I want to thank you for getting her and Julia such a good deal on this place," Melanie said kindly.

"I did tell you that Melanie is my financial wizard, didn't I, Lauren?"

"Sure you did. We spoke once during the transaction, I think," said Lauren.

"We did. I remember," Melanie said.

"Mimi, can you help me?" Ava said, walking up and taking Melanie's hand.

"Sure, honey. Just a sec." She turned to Lauren and said, "It's so nice to meet you. I'll be right back."

Lauren nodded and watched her walk away with a smile on her face.

"So what's the deal, Lauren?" asked Krista.

"What do you mean?" Lauren asked innocently.

"You haven't given Melanie one appraising look. I'm not sure you ever gave Brooke a genuine smile like you just did Melanie," said Krista. She saw Julia, standing next to Lauren, trying not to smirk.

"She's the one. There's no need to do anything but love her because she loves you. It's obvious," Lauren stated.

"Brooke loved me," Krista contended.

"Yeah, but not like Melanie does and not like you love her."

"How can you tell? You haven't even talked to her for five minutes."

"I've talked to you!" Lauren said. "When you and Julia talk about working here in the summers, the woman with the kids always comes up. If you could see the look on your face! It's crystal clear you were in love with her and still are. And the way she looks at you, with certainty and security, well, I hope someone looks at me that way someday."

Krista hugged Lauren and held on for a moment. "Someone will look at you like that someday," she whispered in her ear.

Lauren nodded and then said, "Where's my drink? I thought this was a party."

Heidi handed her a glass of wine. "Here you go."

"Thanks Heidi. I hope Julia appreciates you," she said, giving Julia a teasing look.

"Always causing trouble," Julia said, smirking.

"Speaking of trouble, I have arrived," Tara said, strolling up to the group, holding out her arms.

Tara Holloway held a special place in Krista's heart. She may have been her ex, but they were also friends. Tara always had her back and was as outspoken as she was beautiful. Her acting skills were highly regarded and she was still sought after even though she was in her fifties. She had an award winning performance in Ten Queens' debut film that brought respect to their brand-new undertaking.

Ten Queens had come to life after ten women spent a week together at Lovers Landing. They were actresses, directors, producers; Brooke was their writer, and Julia ran the business. Their focus was on female-led movies and series with a same-sex influence. They wanted to show the gay community in a positive light and as ordinary everyday people, just like in real life.

"What are you doing here? The meeting isn't until next week!" Krista said, hugging her friend.

"I heard you were having a party. My invitation must have been misplaced," she said, quirking an eyebrow.

Krista chuckled. "The party is for family. I can't imagine what happened to yours because you are definitely family."

Tara grinned. "You always have the best lines of bullshit."

Krista grinned and noticed Tara looking past her. She turned and saw Melanie walking toward them.

"Oh my, my," Tara said. "Beautiful as always, Melanie. Damn woman, do you age?"

"Hi Tara. Always nice to see you," Melanie said graciously, putting her arm around Krista possessively.

Krista snickered and shook her head. Out of the corner of her eye she saw Julia holding in a laugh.

"Look at you two," Tara said, holding out her arms. "All I can say is…it's about fucking time!" She put her arms around both of them in a group hug. When they pulled away Tara said sincerely, "I'm really happy for you both."

"Thanks," Krista said, beaming. "I've got some people I'd really like for you to meet."

"Oh yeah?"

"Yeah, they're my family," Krista said proudly.

She took Lauren and Tara and introduced them to the kids and to Stephanie, Heather, and Jennifer.

"This one I know," Tara said, hugging Courtney. "Where's your sister?"

"Right behind you," Becca said, grinning.

Krista looked around the room and loudly said, "All the big

people come with me." She looked at the kids and said, "Chef has something special planned for you kids." She grabbed Melanie by the hand and led them back to the bar.

She looked out at the people gathered in the room and saw family and friends that meant the world to her waiting for her to speak. "Melanie and I wanted to have this party to celebrate. It took us long enough to finally figure this out," she said, squeezing her love's hand. "Or, as Tara astutely pointed out, it's about fucking time!"

The crowd laughed and agreed with her.

"We've decided a few things and wanted to share them with y'all," Krista began. Melanie chuckled next to her as Krista's Texas accent slipped out.

"We're going to use Lovers Landing as our home base and move into Cabin 5," she said, smiling at Julia.

Julia nodded at her decision and said, "It's just the right size."

"We're going to help Becca and Julia the rest of the summer with the groups at Lovers Landing," Melanie said, picking up where Krista left off.

"Oh cool!" said Becca. "That'll be fun. Courtney will be here too."

Krista saw a quick smile on Courtney's face and then she gazed over toward Jennifer. *Something is definitely happening there*, she thought.

Then her eyes met Tara's. She pinned Krista with a look, but didn't say anything.

"So does that mean we're getting the old gang back together?" Heidi asked, grinning.

"It does. I hope you're ready," said Melanie. "There's no telling what we'll get into this time."

The group laughed and Krista continued. "We've decided not to get married," she said, looking at Melanie and holding her hand.

"Why not?" several people said.

Melanie looked at Krista. "Our hearts married years ago." Then she looked out at their family and friends and added, "It just took a while for the other parts of us to catch up."

"But," Krista said, as everyone looked at her, "we were married on June 4th, 1991 so we are celebrating that as our anniversary now."

"That's only a few days away," said Stephanie.

Krista and Melanie looked at one another, just then realizing it was indeed a few days away.

Melanie laughed. "Wow, time flies when you're in love. We started this thirty-two years ago. Steph was eight and Jenn was seven. Neither one of us could let the other go completely and this is why." She looked intently at Krista. "You helped me raise the girls even though you didn't live with us in the same house, so don't ever doubt these are your girls too, along with your grandchildren."

Tears stung Krista's eyes. "You're making me cry again." She took a breath and said, "Anyway, we just wanted all of you to know what we're doing together. We'll always be together."

"Lita, you're crying again," Kyle said, walking into the room. "I thought you were dancing with Mimi."

Krista whirled around and said happily, "We were waiting on you." She scooped him up. "Where's the DJ?"

"I'm here," said Becca, grabbing her phone and the music began again through the speakers.

29

Tara found Krista later and said, "I'm not surprised you're staying here. You always liked this place, but what about our next project? You're not retiring from the Ten Queens, are you? I'm not sure the others will like that."

"Is that why you gave me that look when we were catching everyone up?"

"I'm not sure you realize how much the others depend on you. After all, this was your idea," Tara said.

"Just because it's my idea doesn't mean I run things. We all have a part. That being said, I'm not as motivated as I was."

Tara chuckled. "What does that mean?"

"I don't give a shit," Krista said flatly.

"Yes you do."

"I really don't. When Brooke walked away from me, it ended my affair with Hollywood and my heart was broken so I damn sure didn't want to be entertaining happy couples here. I found solace in that little cabin by the lake. Because I am a responsible person I found two scripts that would be good for the company. Seriously, I'm done."

Tara narrowed her eyes and said, "Are you sure?"

Krista searched the room until her eyes fell on Melanie. She was in an animated discussion with Heidi. Krista knew this was one of her favorite things and it showed in her delighted face. "Look at her, Tara," Krista said, nodding toward Melanie. "We let too many things get in the way of us being together. Never again. Melanie is all I want. We have so much living to do and it has nothing to do with Hollywood or keeping secrets. I'll keep this place open as long as Julia and Becca want because there will always be women afraid to come out. But there are no more secrets between or about Melanie and me."

"That look in your eyes tells me you have a plan to share with the company," Tara said, smiling slyly.

"You'd be right, but that's enough business talk. You never did tell me why you're here early."

"I wanted to see for myself that you were okay. You haven't been very good at answering texts or phone calls."

"Uh-huh, and?"

"And I might want to look at property in the area, so I called Lauren."

Krista gave Tara a harsh look. "I thought we talked about Lauren. She is off limits."

"No, *you* talked about Lauren. Calm the fuck down. She's my friend. That's all. My straight Texas friend."

"It's taken her three years to end her marriage with Marcus and it was hard on the whole family. They are both good people, but different people than they were in high school."

"Aren't we all?"

"You know what I mean. They grew apart."

"Is Brooke coming to the meeting?" asked Tara, changing the subject.

"Hold up," Krista said, raising her hand. "Are you serious about property around here? You know you are welcome to any of the cabins at any time."

"Thanks, but I've grown fond of the slow living around here."

Krista gave her a skeptical look.

"Honestly Krissy." She chuckled. "I like it here."

"Okay," she said suspiciously.

"You didn't answer my question. Is Brooke going to be here?"

"As far as I know she will. Now, this is a party, let's dance," Krista said, getting up.

Tara started to walk off when Krista stopped her. "Where are you going?"

"I'm not dancing with you. I'm dancing with Lauren," she said, grinning and walking away.

Melanie walked up and Krista shook her head as the smile grew on her face. "Tara Holloway is definitely trouble."

"She knows she'd be in trouble if she tried to dance with you," Melanie said, taking Krista's hand and leading her to the dance floor.

"When did you get a jealous streak?"

"I've always had it with Tara, you know that," Melanie said, dancing them away from the others and nibbling Krista's ear.

"That was years ago," Krista said, leaning her head back so Melanie had access to her neck.

"You have no idea how hot my jealousy burned when I knew you were with someone else," Melanie said, biting Krista's neck.

Krista pulled back. "You always said you didn't want me to be alone."

"That doesn't mean I liked it when you were with other women."

Krista gave Melanie a sexy smile. "What other secrets have you been keeping?"

Melanie chuckled. "I told you there were things we never said."

Krista's face softened. "I'm sorry. I had no idea."

"I know how you can make it up to me," Melanie said, her voice low.

Krista looked around and made sure no one was looking and snuck them out the side door to the bar and into her office.

Melanie said, laughing, "Do you think we'll be missed?"

"We'll be back," Krista said, locking the door.

* * *

The next morning Krista and Melanie were sitting on their patio when Jennifer walked up.

"Hey," Krista said, hopping up and giving her a hug. She looked behind Jennifer and then said, "You're alone?'

"I know, that doesn't happen very often." She chuckled.

"You okay, sweetie?" Melanie asked, concern in her voice.

"Yeah... I know we're supposed to go back tomorrow, but I wondered if you'd mind if I stayed a few extra days," Jennifer said tentatively.

"Sure. You can stay as long as you like. The boys will love that." Krista grinned.

"Actually, the boys are going back with Steph and Heather. Their dad–" She rolled her eyes and blew out a breath. "I don't know why I do that. Brandt is picking them up at Steph's for the rest of the month."

"He has them all month?" Melanie said, surprised. "That's not how you usually do it."

"I know. He wants to take them on two separate trips and it will be easier this way. I'll still see them on weekends," she explained. "Let me put it this way, I agreed to *try* this."

Melanie nodded and Krista smiled tenderly at Jennifer. "I know it's hard. I can remember that summer when you'd go see your dad and grandparents. I missed you."

Jennifer looked up. "Really?"

"Yes." Krista nodded. "I know it sounds silly since I barely knew you. I think I not only had a connection with your mom but with you and Steph, too. That's another reason I couldn't let y'all go."

"That is oddly comforting, Krissy. I hate it when the boys are gone."

"I hated it when you were gone, too," said Melanie.

Jennifer smiled at her mom and then looked at Krista. "I've been thinking a lot about our conversation the other day. You said before we got here that you had made up your mind that you were through with relationships."

"I did. I was done," she said, smiling at Melanie. "I did that because I knew my heart couldn't take another hurt."

"But then you saw Mom."

"Your mom is my heart, Jenny. When I saw her–" Krista paused as tears immediately sprang to her eyes and a lump formed in her throat. Melanie reached for her hand and squeezed. "Whew, it is still overwhelming when I think about seeing your mom on that dock. Anyway, when I did, my heart stopped, then constricted like someone was squeezing it," she said, holding up her hand and making a fist. "Then it started beating out of my chest because I knew everything was going to be all right."

"Really?"

"Yes. I didn't know how, but my heart knew it was home and from that moment it was healed."

"You've been through a lot more than I have, but I haven't wanted or even thought about being with another person since Brandt left. It's been four years and I really thought my heart couldn't feel anymore."

"But," Melanie gently encouraged her daughter.

"But I've felt a spark for someone," she said shyly as a smile grew on her face.

Krista grinned at her. "Could it be a certain goddaughter of mine?"

Jennifer nodded. "I figured you knew."

"We know because the two of you laugh and look happy around one another and with the boys," said Melanie.

"I've never been with a woman before," she blurted out.

"Everyone has a first time, Jenn," Krista said affectionately.

"I've only been with Krista," Melanie said, looking at her daughter with such love.

"What?" Krista said, sitting up straight. "You said there was a woman in college."

"There was, but I only kissed her."

Krista narrowed her eyes at Melanie. "You made me believe I was not your first."

"Well duh. Honey, I have two kids," Melanie teased.

"You know what I mean," Krista said, exasperated.

Melanie grinned at her and then turned back to Jennifer. "I was more excited than nervous." Melanie looked up, trying to find the words. "I wanted all of Krista and in every way. I can't explain it. I didn't just want her, I wanted to give myself to her, too."

Jennifer nodded. "I get it, Mom. But you know I am older than she is," she said, wincing.

Krista chuckled. "Believe me, that doesn't matter to Courtney just as it didn't matter to me. I remember thinking, here's this gorgeous woman who has her shit together and could have anyone, but she wants me. I still can't believe it!"

"Oh darlin'," Melanie drawled to Krista.

"I can't have anyone I want," Jennifer said.

"Yes you can. You're just like your Mom; she didn't realize it either."

Jennifer nodded and thought about what they both said.

"Can I add one thing?" Krista asked.

"Is this one of the life lessons Courtney's been telling me about?" Jennifer asked.

Krista furrowed her brow. "Maybe. Seriously, if you think there is something between you and Courtney, don't let anything get in the way."

"Like we did," added Melanie. "Go for it! We'll help in any way you need us. Remember that."

"Okay. Thanks," Jennifer said, finally relaxing a little. "There is something about her that makes me want to know more. I did think about y'all and decided to be brave," she said, using the word that Krista kept saying she wished she had back then. "The timing couldn't be better since the boys will be with their dad. I'm taking vacation next week, but I can still work from here if need be."

"Good for you," Krista said firmly.

"I don't want to get in your way. I know you have a business meeting this week that Courtney said she had to help with and then your anniversary is a few days away."

"You're never in our way," Melanie said.

"Well…" Krista said playfully.

Jennifer and Melanie laughed.

"Courtney doesn't have to help with the meeting. Julia and I can manage without her if y'all want to go somewhere."

"Oh no, we don't want to go anywhere. This place was magical for y'all. We want some of that."

Krista chuckled. "Well then, let's go have one more magical day with the whole family."

30

"Where have you been?" Krista said, bending down to pick up the multicolored cat. She nestled the orange, black, brown and white beauty to her chest and she instantly began to purr. Krista chuckled. "That's my girl."

Melanie reached over to pet the cat and could feel her purring. "You make all the women purr, don't you, darlin'," she said, smirking.

"You are the only woman that makes me purr," Krista said, kissing her on the cheek.

Melanie smiled down at the cat and sighed.

"What's wrong?" Krista said. "Are you nervous to meet everyone?"

"Not really. It's just, are you sure this is what you want? Just because I retired doesn't mean I expect you to," she said earnestly.

"I'm positive, Mel. I haven't been this excited about something since I bought this place."

"Excited about what?" Jennifer asked, walking up with Courtney.

"Excited to live with your mom and wake up with her every day and plan new adventures," Krista said, putting the cat down and putting her arms around Melanie's neck.

"It's okay, Sappho," Courtney said, picking up the cat. "You're not the only one purring around here," she said playfully to Krista.

"Be careful with those comments, my dear goddaughter," Krista said menacingly. "Because I'm quite sure I'm not the only one purring."

"Well, duh," Jennifer said. "This is a resort full of lesbians," she said, trying to deflect Krista's aim from them.

"True," Krista chuckled. Then she eyed them both with one arm still around Melanie. "What are y'all up to today?"

"Becca texted and said they are five minutes out. We thought we'd help take the queens to their cabins," said Courtney.

Krista looked at Jennifer and said, "So she put you to work?"

Jennifer smiled. "I don't mind helping."

"They've all been here so many times they know where they're going. All you have to do is tell them which golf cart is theirs," said Krista.

"Maybe I wanted to introduce a friend to Allison and Libby," said Courtney.

"Oh," Krista said, nodding. Allison Jennings and Libby Scott had become the new power couple in Hollywood after Brooke Bell, the journalist turned screenwriter, had written a beautiful coming out piece about their twenty-year closeted relationship in Hollywood.

They were all at Lovers Landing three years ago when Krista thought Brooke was trying to sneak into the resort and out their hideaway and the people there. Krista boldly invited Brooke to come visit as her guest. She thought if she could show Brooke what Lovers Landing really meant to the women that came there then she wouldn't out them.

Allison, Libby and four other women were there that fateful week and not only did Brooke not write the story, but they all banded together to form a production company that they could all be proud of and make the content they wanted. Their first movie won the Academy Award for Best Picture, Brooke won for Best Screenplay, Allison won for Best Actress, Tara won for best supporting actress and Megan Easterling, another member of the team, won for Best Director.

When Brooke came to Lovers Landing as Krista's guest she was vulnerable. Krista could see a woman that was slowly self-destructing and wanted to help her. They fell in love and worked closely the next three years while getting the movie made. Three months ago when the entire group met at Lovers Landing to celebrate the awards was when Krista's foolhardy idea for them to get married imploded. At the time it was horrible, but of course it ended up being the best thing that could have happened to both of them.

Now the whole group was coming back together for their annual meeting to discuss ongoing projects and any new ideas or scripts they wanted to pursue. It would be the first time Krista would face her friends and Brooke since the wedding fiasco.

"And maybe we both wanted to be here for you, Krissy," said Jennifer.

Krista smiled at them both, realizing they were here to support her. "Thanks," Krista said, tilting her head. "Brooke won't be here until tomorrow. She's coming just for the meeting."

Courtney nodded. "She's not staying?"

"No. She and Sandra have plans after the meeting," Krista explained.

"Sandra?" Courtney asked. "Is she the girl from high school?"

"She's the one."

"I guess Brooke will feel awkward being here," Courtney said as if she'd just thought of it.

"Probably. We've been texting and I'll be able to talk to everyone else tonight before the meeting, so hopefully it won't be too bad." Krista looked at Melanie and said, "She was brave to do what she did."

"Unlike us over the years," Melanie said with her arm around Krista. "But no more."

"That's right, not any more," Krista added.

"I don't know why I didn't think of this sooner, but honey, do you think Brooke would want to bring Sandra with her? While y'all have your meeting she could go with us out on the lake," Melanie said.

"Yeah," Courtney said excitedly. "Maybe Brooke wouldn't feel so awkward then, but would you, Krissy?"

"Not at all. Let's get everyone settled in and I'll call her," Krista said as Becca pulled up in the van.

Julia stepped out of the van first and gave Krista a grin. "They are ready to dance and sing."

Krista took a deep breath and chuckled. "Help us all."

"Krista!" Megan exclaimed, jumping off the bus. She ran over and hugged Krista and then held her at arm's length with a serious look on her face. "Julia said you were better than okay."

Krista chuckled. "Julia would be right."

Megan then noticed Melanie standing next to Krista, radiating confidence with a relaxed grace. "Good for you," she said, nodding at Melanie.

Megan's partner Renee Oliver greeted Krista next, followed by the producers in the group, Anna Cain and Shelley Haskell.

Libby Scott hugged Krista tightly and whispered in her ear, "I'm so happy for you."

"Thanks Libby, me too. I'll introduce you as soon as your wife gets off the bus," Krista said.

Allison Jennings stepped toward Krista with her eyes narrowed. "You look better today than you did five years ago," she said, pulling Krista into a hug.

Krista rolled her eyes. "Thanks Allison. You may have won more than one Oscar, but I know you're lying."

Before Allison could protest Krista said, "Hey everyone, I know Julia filled you in on the last few months. I want you to meet the woman who's always had my heart, but we somehow managed to always make things harder than they had to be. No more." Krista put her arm around Melanie. "This is Melanie Zimmer," she said, kissing her cheek.

Each woman greeted Melanie as if they'd known her for years. Then Courtney corralled them all to their golf carts, introducing Jennifer as the women climbed into their carts. They agreed to meet back in the restaurant in an hour.

As they walked into their cabin Krista turned to Melanie and wrapped her arms around her. "That wasn't too bad was it?"

"Not at all," Melanie said. "They seemed thrilled to see you happy and I don't think Allison was lying. You are beautiful, my love."

Krista kissed her gently. "You make me beautiful."

"Mmm," Melanie said, returning her kiss. "Why don't you call Brooke and then we can continue this discussion."

"Such a good idea," Krista said.

"I'll just wait in here," Melanie said, walking into the bedroom.

Krista pulled her phone out and scrolled to Brooke in her contacts. She hit the button to connect the call and waited.

Brooke picked up and said, "Krista?"

"Hey Brooke," Krista said tentatively. This was only the second time she'd talked to Brooke since she'd walked out of their wedding. Their communication had been limited to text messages and emails since then. "Did you and Sandra make it to Dallas?"

"Yeah, we're here. Is everything all right?"

"Yes, everybody is here. Listen, Melanie was wondering if Sandra would like to come with you tomorrow. While we're meeting, she, her daughter and Courtney are going out on the lake. I know you're going to feel awkward when you get here and Sandra being with you might be nice," Krista said, realizing she was rambling. "Shit, I'm sorry Brooke."

Brooke chuckled. "It's all right. I know this is weird."

"I'd really like to talk to you for a few minutes before the meeting. I need to thank you, Brooke."

"Thank me?"

"Yeah. Will you come a little early tomorrow and bring Sandra?"

"Hold on," Brooke said.

Krista could hear her muffled voice and then she came back on the call.

"Okay Krista. Sandra said that would be nice. I've told her how wonderful Courtney and Becca are, so she'd like to meet them, as well as you."

"Wow," Krista breathed. "Is this strange to you?"

"Yes and no," Brooke laughed. "Tell me, are you happy?"

"More than I ever dreamed."

"Me too, so this doesn't have to be weird," Brooke said. "I'll see you tomorrow."

"Okay Brooke, see you tomorrow," Krista said, ending the call.

She was smiling when she walked into the bedroom.

* * *

The next morning Krista was getting things together for the meeting when Melanie came out of the bedroom and walked up behind her. She put her arms around her middle and pulled her to her chest.

"What's this?" Krista asked, leaning back into her.

"Just a little love," she said, kissing her neck. "It was fun to see you with your friends last night."

"I don't know that I'd call them friends. I mean we do work together and have fun when we all get together, but Tara is the only one I'd really call a friend."

"They all seemed very invested in our relationship. I don't know how many of them told me they knew you and Brooke wouldn't work out."

"Exactly! Why didn't they speak up before?"

"Would you have listened?"

"I doubt it." Krista chuckled. "We'll see how happy they are with me when I tell them I'm leaving." Krista spun around in Melanie's arms and put a finger to her lips. "And before you ask, yes I'm sure this is what I want. Because you are what I want and being with you is what I'm doing."

Melanie kissed her quickly, shutting her up. "Got it." She grinned. "We'd better get going. You don't want Brooke and Sandra to wonder where we are."

"I love you, Mel," Krista said seriously, not letting her go.

"I love you too, Kris. Where did that come from?"

"I think it's nice you want to take Sandra out while we're meeting."

Melanie smiled. "We have all taken a very long road to get to where we want to be. There's no reason for her to sit in a hotel room when she could be enjoying this beautiful resort you and Julia built and that I now work at," she said, kissing Krista again. "Come on." She took her hand and they walked out to the golf cart.

They pulled up to the office just as an unfamiliar car parked by the front door. Krista got out of the golf cart and smiled at Brooke as she got out of the car.

"Wow," she exclaimed. "I've never seen you look so calm and carefree," Krista said with a broad smile. "Sorry, you know how I babble sometimes." She cringed.

Brooke laughed. "Yeah you do, especially when you're nervous."

"I'd like you to meet Melanie," Krista said, taking Melanie's hand.

"And I'd like you to meet Sandra," Brooke said, mirroring Krista's movement.

Melanie and Sandra looked at one another and laughed. Brooke and Krista joined in.

"Okay, I'm going to say it; this is a little weird," Krista said.

"It is, but not really. Look at you," Brooke said sweetly. "You look more beautiful than I've ever seen you."

"Now that we've established how wonderful you both look, there's something to be said for being where you belong," said Melanie.

"And now that you both are where your hearts want you to be," Sandra said, speaking up. "It looks good on you. *Both* of you."

Brooke beamed at her girlfriend. "Sandra is a counselor and knows her shit."

Krista burst out laughing. "My God, I know six women that will need you later."

Brooke laughed with her. "I know that's right."

"Come on, let's go to our cabin so we can talk," Krista said, leading them to the golf cart.

She took them to the cabin and Brooke got out, looking around. "It's nice over here."

"Yeah it is," Krista answered. "It's a smaller cabin, but I really like it here." She looked at Melanie.

"I wonder why?" Brooke teased. She turned to Melanie and asked, "Isn't Krista's cabin the one you originally stayed in?"

"Yes. It's a lot different now, but the bones are the same," Melanie said. "Would you like something to drink?"

"I'd love some water," Sandra said.

Melanie went inside and got her a bottle of water. They sat out on the patio where a cool morning breeze greeted them.

"I wanted to talk to you about a few things before the meeting, but first I want to thank you," Krista said to Brooke.

"Thank me? For what?"

"For stopping us. For being brave enough to stop my idiotic idea."

"Krista," Brooke started.

Sandra interrupted her. "If you're thanking Brooke then I want to thank you for encouraging her to reach out. I'm not sure she would have done that without you."

Melanie looked around the table and smiled. "You know, we're all where we should be and where we always wanted to be. Yes, there were lots of tears and hurt hearts, but Krista and I have finally made it back to one another and we're celebrating."

Brooke smiled, then reached out and held Sandra's hand. "And we don't have to keep any secrets!"

Krista chuckled, holding Melanie's hand. "That's right. No more secrets."

Melanie's phone pinged and she pulled it out of her pocket and read the message. She looked at Sandra and said, "Courtney and Jennifer are at the dock and ready when we are."

"All I need to do is change," Sandra said.

"Right this way," Melanie said, leading them into the house.

A few minutes later they came out and Melanie said, "I told them to come pick us up so you'll have the golf cart for your meeting. Good luck," she said, bending down and kissing Krista softly.

"See you later, hon," Sandra said, kissing Brooke.

When they left Brooke looked at Krista and narrowed her eyes. "What are you about to do, Krissy?"

"That's why I wanted to talk to you," Krista answered.

31

Brooke walked into the meeting with Krista and everyone turned to look at them.

She looked at Krista sideways and grinned.

"Hey everyone. Sorry I missed last night's party. I heard it was something," she said, smiling at the others. "Krista and I wanted to thank you all for being part of our disastrous wedding a few months ago," she added as they both shook their heads and laughed, trying to put the others at ease.

Krista said, "We are happily with the people we should've been with all along. You know how lesbians and love goes." She held up her hands playfully.

"I'd love for you all to meet Sandra after the meeting. Right now she's out with Melanie enjoying the lake while we find amazing new movies to make," Brooke said.

"Well then," said Allison. "Let's get to it, so we can join them."

Krista looked at Brooke and nodded, happy that the awkwardness was gone.

Julia, the chief financial officer, gave them a quick rundown on their financial position. "I know you don't like to deal with the money part of things, but we're in good shape. The series we sold to Netflix is set to debut in September. So, who's next?"

They all took turns updating the group on anything they had coming up or ideas for new content.

Krista went last to discuss the new projects she hoped they'd like. "I've found two scripts that were emailed to all of you a few days ago. Either one of these could be the next winner for us. There are roles that Brooke can adapt to Allison, Libby, Tara, and Renee. Anna and Shelley will have fun with either one and Megan," Krista said, looking at their director, "both of these reminded me of stories you mentioned being interested in."

"I read them and want to suggest..." Megan said, looking around the table. "We do them both!" she exclaimed.

Renee laughed. "She's been so excited about both that she couldn't choose which one we should do. I have to agree. There are great roles for all of us. Good job finding these, Krista."

"I read them, too. I'm just going to put it out there, are we looking for pictures for us to star in or that are important to the gay community today? Because those characters could be younger and the story more relevant without us in them," said Tara daringly.

"Are you ready to retire, Tara?" asked Allison.

"Not necessarily, but you know how roles dwindle. I'm in my fifties and you're not far behind. I'm not trying to be a bitch. I'm trying to stay true to why we formed Ten Queens in the first place."

"Let's do both and make one with us and one with younger actors," offered Libby.

"That's not a bad idea," said Krista. "But before we decide you need to know that I'm limiting my role in the company to a consulting position."

"What exactly does that mean?" asked Anna. She, Shelley and Krista had worked closely on the day to day problems while organizing and filming the movie.

Allison smirked at Krista. "It means she wants to go live her happily-ever-after with Melanie."

"Oh," said Libby. "Melanie is retired so now you're retired too?"

"Not exactly. We're going to work at Lovers Landing all summer," said Krista.

"Right," said Allison. "And who do you suggest take over your role? You did so much to make the movie happen between filming and publicity. Who knew you were such a business woman?"

Krista smiled. "Thank you, I think," she said cautiously. "My assistant Presley will take over my role, with your approval. Believe me, she is so much better at this than I am."

"I can verify that," said Brooke.

"She is quite good, but this is a lot bigger, Krissy," said Tara.

"She was born for this, Tara."

"Okay. I know you wouldn't run out on us unless you left us with someone better," she said sarcastically.

"I'm not running out on you!" Krista said defensively.

"I think she's had her fill of Hollywood and now it's time to play," teased Libby.

"It's your time," said Brooke. "I wouldn't be happy now if it wasn't for Krista. And Allison, you and Libby wouldn't be enjoying your life out and proud right now. What about all the couples that have been to Lovers Landing since Krista and Julia opened it? Hell yes, Krista, go live your life with your love."

"Damn! How passionate," said Renee. "I knew you could write the words, Brooke, but you can speak them, too."

"Let's give Presley a shot," said Julia, who had been quiet during the discussion. "She's done a great job screening people for us and running Krista's business."

"Okay, I'm for it," said Allison.

The others agreed and then Shelley said, "Hey wait. Does that mean we're not meeting here anymore?"

"Y'all are welcome here anytime and I'll still be involved, so yes, we'll still have meetings here."

"Then let's go to the cliffs. I'm ready to jump!" said Megan.

"Meet on the dock in fifteen minutes," Julia said.

Everyone jumped up and gathered their things. Krista turned to Brooke. "Thanks for what you said to the others."

"It's the truth. I really don't know where I'd be if it hadn't been for you and this place," said Brooke.

Krista happily sighed. "I'm glad. Isn't it amazing how much better it feels when you're with the one you're supposed to be with?"

"I feel settled, Krista. Before, I always wondered when something was going to happen to ruin everything, you know?"

"I remember. We talked about that so many times."

"I know and now I know why. Please believe me, I never wanted to hurt you, but I always felt like there was a piece of you I'd never get. You held something back and I knew it was Melanie, but I also didn't know how to tell you. I figured that was the way it was supposed to be," Brooke explained. "But when I saw Sandra again for the first time I understood. I didn't know it, but I was holding back too. We were destined for that wreck of a wedding and maybe we had to go through that to find our happiness. You found it with Melanie, right?"

"I have. It's always been there, we just had to be brave enough to hold onto it," Krista said.

"Then let's be brave and jump off a cliff with our loves," Brooke said, smiling.

"Let's go!" Krista exclaimed.

* * *

The next day Krista, Melanie and Julia waited at the van as the others loaded their things and said goodbye.

"I'm glad Courtney and Jennifer are going with Becca to take that rowdy bunch back to the airport," said Julia.

"Me too! It was my turn to go with Becca," Krista chuckled.

Allison walked up to Krista and hugged her. "Another successful meeting at Lovers Landing." She looked at Melanie and said, "Welcome to this dysfunctional family of ours. I've been trying to recall where I've met you before."

Melanie tilted her head and waited.

"It was after Krista's break-up with Tara. I remember seeing you with Krista at a small party and thinking to myself that you suited her. I wish now that I'd spoken up, but no matter, you're together now and that's what's important," Allison said.

"I hope you and Libby will be back soon," said Krista.

"We'll see," said Allison, evasive as ever.

Krista shook her head and chuckled. "Allison is such a diva," she whispered to Melanie.

"You can say that again," Julia said, just as quietly.

They waved as the van left and Julia said, "Heidi is waiting for us at the dock."

"What?"

"Yep, it's just us four and we have important things to discuss," said Julia seriously.

"We do?" said Krista.

"Yes," Julia said, putting her arm around Melanie. "What's this about your daughter dating my daughter?"

Melanie's eyebrows climbed her forehead and Krista guffawed.

"What are you laughing at?" Julia said. "She's your daughter too!"

Krista stood a little straighter and said, "She is!"

They spent the rest of the day together just as they had all those years ago.

32

"This has been the best day," Krista said.

"Do you think it's because it's our anniversary?" asked Melanie, squeezing Krista's hand.

"That's part of it, but no one else is here. Julia and Heidi are taking a few days to themselves. Courtney took Jennifer back to Houston and Becca is off with her boyfriend until the next group gets here."

"Was it okay to spend our first real anniversary together with no one else around?"

"Yes!" exclaimed Krista. "We've done all the things we love. We rode bikes this morning, went out on the lake, and hiked up to what is now our official hideout."

"We cooked together, which we're getting to do more and more. Took a very pleasant nap," Melanie said suggestively.

"That was an awfully nice nap," Krista said, her voice low and sexy.

"And now, we're walking in the moonlight to our home."

"Our home? Is that what you want to call our little cabin?"

"That's what it is. If you think about it, it's the first place we've been able to call home together," said Melanie.

"Home is an interesting word because for me whenever I was with you I felt like I was home," Krista said, squeezing Melanie's hand.

"For me, I always dreamed that we could live together in our own place, our home."

"Then honey, we're home," Krista said as they walked onto the patio. "I have one more thing I want us to do on our anniversary." She grabbed a blanket that was on the table and took Melanie's hand. She led them out to their little beach and spread the blanket on the grass.

"What a perfect night for stargazing," Melanie said, helping to spread the blanket.

They settled next to one another and looked up at the night sky. The stars were bright and twinkling and the moon was waning. There was a soft breeze floating through the trees and they could hear the water lapping up to the sand.

"What did Jennifer say about Courtney today when you talked to her?" Krista asked.

"She said they are still figuring things out. There is a definite connection and Courtney is looking into schools in the area."

"Good for them. Even if it doesn't work out, at least they're giving it a chance."

"That's exactly what I told her."

"We may have a new neighbor," said Krista.

"Who?"

"Tara has been looking at property on the lake," Krista said.

"Really," Melanie said thoughtfully. "You know, she seems to really like Lauren."

"I know," Krista said unenthusiastically.

"Why do you say it like that?"

"Because I care for both of them and I want to believe that Tara is changing, but Lauren is vulnerable and I know she's curious about being with a woman."

"They could just be friends," Melanie said.

"Do you believe that?"

"I don't know. I haven't known Lauren long, but I think she can take care of herself. She may be curious about women, but I think Tara has met her match."

Krista chuckled. "We'll see. Tara's gone back to LA for now. Who knows what mischief she'll get into back there."

Melanie looked over at Krista and said, "Do you remember looking at the stars that summer?"

Krista smiled at her. "I remember thinking silently to myself while we were on that blanket thirty-two years ago that I hope I get to do this many more times with you." She rolled onto her side and looked into Melanie's warm, soft brown eyes. "I can't remember ever looking up at the stars over the years and not thinking of you, if only for a moment. And when we were apart, if I was missing you more than usual I'd look up at the stars and wonder if you were looking too." She reached her hand out and cupped Melanie's face. "I always thought I wanted what Julia and Heidi have, but that's not what I wanted. What I really wanted was you and Steph and Jenn. I thought I wanted to be married with kids, but I wanted you and our kids. It's so clear to me now. All along, all I wanted was you." With tears in her eyes, she leaned in and tenderly kissed Melanie. She took a shaky breath. "My heart is so full and I have the forever I always dreamed of," she said, kissing Melanie again.

"Our souls have found the ones they love. Ours is a never-ending love story," Melanie said, kissing Krista and sealing their promises once again.

EIGHTEEN YEARS LATER

Kyle stood on the back deck and looked out over the water. He could hear an engine revving as if it was coming in fast and then it immediately quieted.

"That's probably them coming in off the lake. Come on," he said, holding out his hand to his boyfriend Oliver.

"I'm a little nervous. I mean, both your moms seem to like me okay, but I know how much you love your grandmothers," Oliver said, squeezing Kyle's hand.

"Mimi and Lita will love you, just like I do," Kyle said, swinging their hands then stopping. "Well, not like I do, but you know what I mean."

Oliver laughed. "I know you're trying to calm me down."

Kyle grinned at him as they stepped onto the walkway and watched a jet ski pull into the slot at the end of the dock.

"Your grandmothers are on a jet ski," said Oliver, surprised.

"Yeah, Lita got it for Mimi a couple of years ago on her eightieth birthday," Kyle said nonchalantly. "Mimi's the one driving, Lita's holding on because she can't keep her hands off my Mimi," he deadpanned.

"What?" Oliver asked, becoming more surprised by the second.

"They are crazy in love and have been since forever," Kyle said, waving at his grandmothers.

"Wait a minute. You didn't tell me your grandmother is Krista Kyle!" Oliver said, his eyes almost popping out of his head.

"I'm sure I did. I told you I was named after her," Kyle said. "She's just my Lita to me. We did a few Hollywood things and I met some cool people when I was younger, but she's always been just my abuelita."

"We are bingeing her series and watching every one of her movies when we get back to school!" Oliver said.

Kyle grinned at him. "Come on, I'll introduce you."

"Now I'm more nervous than ever. One of your grandmother's rides a jet ski and the other is a famous Hollywood actor. My God, Kyle!"

Kyle laughed. "Hey grandmas!"

"Kyle!" they both exclaimed.

"I'm so glad you're here," Krista said, giving him a hug.

"Come here, my beautiful grandson," Melanie said, hugging him tight.

"Mimi, Lita, this is Oliver," Kyle said, introducing him.

"We are so happy to finally meet you," Krista said.

"And we're so glad you could come to our party," added Melanie.

"Speaking of the party, we've got to run home and change. Will you meet us inside?" Krista asked, reaching for Melanie's hand.

"Of course. Is everyone else here?" asked Kyle.

"I think so. Oliver, it was so nice to meet you," Melanie said as they walked to the golf cart.

"We'll be right back," said Krista.

On the way home Melanie said, "I can't believe we got them all here."

"You can be very persuasive when you want to be, my love," Krista said, putting her arm around Melanie.

"I'm glad Julia and Heidi will be here too."

"I don't think we could have a party without them," Krista said. She pulled into the same cabin they had been living in since Melanie returned to the lake eighteen years ago. They'd discussed building something bigger or remodeling one of the other cabins, but this was their home.

They quickly changed and were about to go back out the door when Melanie grabbed Krista and pulled her in close.

"I love you so much, baby," she said, burying her face in Krista's neck. Her hair had a few more gray streaks now and the wrinkles were a little deeper around her eyes, but that's because she was happy and smiled so often. But those stunning blue eyes were still crystal clear and Melanie's favorite place to fall at the end of the day.

"I love you, my precious darling," Krista said with tears in her eyes.

"Why the tears?" Melanie asked as she kissed them away.

"I'm so, so grateful. All our kids, grandkids, and even our adorable little great-granddaughter are here. But I'm most grateful for you, my love. I'm so glad you came to this lake fifty years ago and we found one another. We have been in love for fifty years and I feel like we're just getting started. You still surprise me in some way every day and that makes me love you even more. I don't know how it's possible, but I do."

Melanie had tears in her eyes when she softly kissed Krista. "I fully intend to surprise you later tonight, too. We'd better go."

Krista chuckled and they walked out hand in hand. When they got to the golf cart, Krista walked around to the driver's side. Melanie followed her and said, "Move over, lover. I want to drive."

Krista grinned and scooted over to the other side. "Lovers, we are certainly that, aren't we baby." She leaned over and kissed Melanie softly and sighed.

The party was in full swing several hours later with music and dancing and plenty of food.

Melanie got everyone's attention and when they quieted she spoke. "Krissy and I want to thank all of you for coming; it means the world to us. We know you are all busy and to indulge a couple of old women with your presence is the best gift you could give us. Now, before we call it a night I need one more dance with my lover," Melanie said, winking at Krista.

Krista couldn't believe Melanie called her that in front of everyone. The first time they made love, when they woke the next morning Krista had called her 'lover' because she'd always wanted to say that. It had become a moment of humor and then one of endearment over the years, but it had only ever been said when they were alone.

Melanie turned to Krista and reached out her hand as the music began to play. Krista listened and then recognized the first song she'd ever sang to Melanie.

"Fifty years ago you sang this song to me and our souls married later that night for all of time. Happy anniversary, my love."

Krista looked around her as they were encircled by their family. She took a moment and could see the love in each face and even a few tears. When she saw Julia smiling at her and then nod she thought this might be the best moment of her life so far.

She wrapped her arms around Melanie's neck and then listened as she sang "Always and Forever." Krista had no doubt that they would be together the rest of this life and beyond because their love was truly never-ending.

ABOUT THE AUTHOR

Small town Texas girl that grew up believing she could do anything. Her mother loved to read and romance novels were a favorite that she passed on to her daughter. She found lesfic novels and her world changed. She not only fell in love with the genre, but wanted to write her own stories. You can find her books on Amazon and her website at jameymoodyauthor.com.

You can email her at jameymoodyauthor@gmail.com

This author is part of iReadIndies, a collective of self-published independent authors of women loving women (WLW) literature. Please visit our website at iReadIndies.com for more information and to find links to the books published by our authors.

As an independent publisher a review is greatly appreciated and I would be grateful if you could take the time to write just a few words.

ALSO BY JAMEY MOODY

Live This Love

The Your Way Series:
Finding Home
Finding Family
Finding Forever

It Takes A Miracle
One Little Yes

The Lovers Landing Series
Where Secrets Are Safe
No More Secrets

JUST FOR YOU

You can get all three romances from The Your Way Series in one book full of love, romance, and happily-ever-afters.

I've included Chapter 1 of Book 1, Finding Home, as a bonus. Enjoy!

Get The Your Way Series.

FINDING HOME
CHAPTER 1

Somedays you're the windshield, somedays you're the bug. At this moment, Frankie Dean felt like the bug. She was going through the mail of Your Way, the fitness center she owned with her two best friends.

"Whatcha got there?" asked Desi. Desdemona Shaw had been Frankie's best friend since kindergarten 40 years ago and one of her partners in the gym. She had short dark hair with hazel eyes that were full of mischief.

"The mail," replied Frankie flatly.

"Duh, I know it's the mail. What are you looking at so intensely?"

Frankie handed Desi the wedding invitation she had been holding.

Desi read it and exclaimed, "What the hell! You have got to be kidding me! She invited you to her wedding?"

"No, she invited all of us, I guess. It's addressed to the gym," Frankie said showing Desi the envelope.

"I can't fucking believe her!" Desi said with fire in her eyes. "Are you all right?" she asked looking at Frankie.

Frankie sighed and said, "Yes, I'm okay. It was a punch to the gut but, I'm over it already." Frankie ran her hand through her short brown hair then continued sorting the mail.

"Are you sure? I'd like to go kick her ass!"

"I'm sure. I promise, I'm over her but, it still pisses me off that I was so stupid. I know better than to date someone that's never been with a woman. It's happened to me twice now and I'm never doing it again!"

"It seems like it's only been a minute since you broke up."

"It's been six months. She'd been seeing him for a month before she told me."

"Typical, they find out what sex is supposed to be like and lose their fucking minds. Now that she knows she'll be telling him what to do but, you just wait, she'll be crawling back."

"Stop, Des, it wasn't like that," Frankie said, her green eyes softening. "Now that it's been six months and I can look at it from a distance, I think Laura really just needed a friend at the time and was lonely. Then I came along and well, you know what happened."

"Yeah, I know. You were kind to her as you are to everyone. I wonder what she would do if we showed up at the wedding?"

"We're not going to the wedding. In her own way I'm sure she was just trying to be nice."

"What wedding are we not going to?" Stella asked, walking into the office. Stella Morris was the third partner in the gym and at 52 looked like a fitness model. Her auburn hair was pulled into a pony tail as she was just finishing teaching a yoga class for beginners.

"Laura sent the gym an invitation to her wedding to the guy she cheated on Frankie with," Desi said, filling Stella in.

"Easy Des," Stella said while placing her arm around Frankie's shoulder. She met Frankie's eyes with her own soft brown ones full of compassion. "Wow, sorry Frankie, I'm sure that had to sting."

"I'm all right, really, you two," Frankie said looking at them both. "I'm happy for her."

"Of course you are because that's the kind of person you are," Stella said.

"Anyway, it's been six months, I've moved on and that's that," Frankie said handing each of them their mail.

"Moved on? You haven't had one date since you broke up," said Desi.

"Exactly, taking a break is a good thing," answered Frankie.

"Maybe for Ross and Rachel but, how is it a good thing for a beautiful, kind, successful, hot lesbian like you?" asked Desi.

"You happen to be a beautiful, kind, successful, hot lesbian, too and I don't see you dating anyone," countered Frankie.

"Oh you two, it doesn't do any good to compare your lesbian hotness," Stella said chuckling. "Besides, Frankie has a strength class in 10 minutes. Go throw some weight around - it always makes me feel better."

"Yep, I'd better go set up," Frankie said walking toward the door. "See y'all later."

"Was that your last class today?" Desi asked Stella.

"Yep, I'm done. Nat has the evening dance class, aren't you doing the evening spin class?"

"Yes, I haven't seen Natalie this afternoon, have you?" Natalie Stevens was their all-around instructor that taught the classes that Stella, Frankie, and Desi didn't cover. She had been with them since almost the beginning. In the 10 years that they had been open, Your Way had become one of the premier fitness centers in town. They specialized in making everyone feel welcome no matter their fitness level, experience, or coordination. There was something for everyone at Your Way.

"She opened this morning, had the afternoon off, and is coming back for that last dance class. That girl would work all day and evening if we'd let her," said Stella.

"That's why I haven't seen her. Frankie and I are closing tonight so I didn't get here until afternoon. Do you think we should go to Laura's wedding?"

"Why would we do that? I know Frankie says she's over her but still, that woman hurt our friend. And I don't care if she didn't mean to."

"I agree. I just don't get it. Frankie is the best girlfriend anyone could have. Laura's crazy for letting her go. I guess I thought she'd see that if we were there."

"It doesn't matter, she's out of Frankie's life and ours too. I'm going home. I've had enough of this place today."

"I expect folks to come by for tours tomorrow, our special with three free one-on-one sessions expires in two days," Desi said, reminding Stella.

"Got it. I'll be ready. See you tomorrow."

* * *

Olivia King stepped off the scale and sighed. She then got in the shower to get ready for work. That number kept rolling through her mind over and over, it reminded her of a slot machine and when it stopped, she wasn't a winner.

As she looked at herself in the mirror she decided today was the day. She'd been hiding all winter and now it was April. One thing she did like about living in Dallas was the weather; not too cold but hot in the summer. She couldn't imagine wearing shorts the way she looked now. She'd had enough.

She finished drying her shoulder length dark blonde hair and pulled her best friend Sofia's name up on her phone, tapped it and waited. This was a good hair day, so at least she had that.

"Good morning," Sofia answered cheerily.

"Hey, I need a favor."

"Okay, OK. Did you get that? OK, your initials," Sofia said chuckling.

"For the millionth time, that is not funny," Olivia responded, rolling her eyes in the mirror.

"Yes it is! Anyway, what do you need?"

"I need you to come with me after work and take a tour of that fitness gym that's running the special," Olivia explained.

"What gym?

"The gym I've told you about the last two weeks," Olivia said sighing. "Do you ever listen to anything I say?"

"Yes, I just needed a reminder. I seem to recall you mentioning something about it."

"Good. I'll pick you up after work."

"Wait, I have plans after work," Sofia said quickly.

"You owe me. I'll be by after work," Olivia said firmly.

"Owe you, why do I owe you?"

"Two weeks ago you begged me to go to that wine bar with you so you could ogle the bartender... who you later disappeared with leaving me there. Or how about this past Saturday when you drug me to karaoke with your co-workers so you could sneak out early with your boss' assistant and no one would notice."

"I'll be ready, what do I need to wear?"

"Your work clothes are fine, we're just taking a tour, not working out."

"Yippee, I can hardly wait," Sofia said sarcastically.

Later that day as Sofia got in Olivia's car she said, "Tell me again why you're doing this."

"Have you looked at me lately? I'm tired of carrying around this extra weight."

"You might need to lose a few pounds but, you don't look bad," said Sofia.

"Gee thanks. I'm never going to get a girlfriend if I don't do something, so I'm joining a gym and losing this weight." Olivia said matter-of-factly.

"You don't expect me to join with you, do you?"

"No. I just wanted you to go with me for the tour."

They walked through the door of Your Way and Frankie greeted them.

"Welcome to Your Way, I'm Frankie, would you let me show you around?"

Sofia eyed Frankie up and down and whispered to Olivia, "I'd let her do more than show me around."

Olivia ignored her and reached out her hand, "Hi, I'm Olivia and this is my friend Sofia."

"Hi Olivia," Frankie said, taking her hand. She looked into the most beautiful brown eyes she'd ever seen. Suddenly realizing she'd been holding Olivia's hand a little longer than she should, Frankie turned to Sofia and said, "Hi Sofia."

"We'd like to take a tour and were interested in the special you're running," said Olivia. What a beautiful woman she thought, her hand tingling where Frankie had held it.

"Great, right this way. We named the gym Your Way because that's exactly what we want you to do, make it yours. Fitness isn't one size fits all, everyone is unique so your plan has to fit you. What do you like to do? We have several different classes, group and individual sessions, as well as sports too."

"Actually, I'm not really sure. That's why I wanted the tour," explained Olivia.

"With the special you get three one-on-one training sessions so I'm sure we can find something you like. And you're welcome to try all the classes to see which you like best or take a different one every time you come in depending on how you feel."

"I know what I'd like to feel," Sofia whispered as they walked to the treadmills.

"Would you stop," Olivia whispered glaring at her friend.

"This area is for the treadmills. If you'll notice, there are TV's at every machine and you can watch whatever you want as you exercise. Right back here is the free weight area. We have plenty of weights, bars, benches and squat racks. Have you ever lifted weights before?" Frankie asked them.

"Not really," Olivia answered.

"No problem. We'll make sure you know how to use these safely so you can get the most from your workout," Frankie said, smiling at Olivia.

At the end of the free weight section was a wall of windows looking into a workout room. "This is where several of our classes are held," Frankie said as Desi walked out of the room.

"This is Desi Shaw, one of the owners," Frankie said, introducing her. "Des, meet Olivia and Sofia. They're taking a tour."

"Hi Olivia, Sofia," Desi said, nodding at each of them. "This is one of two workout spaces that we hold classes in. We have spin classes, kickboxing, HIIT workouts, boot camps, dance, and yoga. When there isn't a class you're welcome to work out in the room with the other equipment."

"Dance?" asked Olivia.

"We have dance fitness classes. They are so much fun. I can't dance to save myself but, I feel like I can when I'm teaching or participating in dance fitness class," said Frankie.

"It's all true, I've seen her dance," Desi said chuckling. "But really, you have to try it at least once. It's a lot of fun. And if there is some other activity that we don't offer, tell us about it, we'll see what we can do."

Desi noticed Frankie looking at the front door intently and turned to see what was happening. In walked Laura, Frankie's ex. Before Desi could stop her she reached the group.

"Excuse me, could I talk to you a minute, Frankie?" Laura asked nervously.

Frankie could feel her face reddening. She hadn't seen Laura in six months and certainly didn't think she'd ever walk back into Your Way. She looked at Olivia and Sofia and smiled.

"Would you excuse me for just a minute? Desi will show the workout room and I'll be right back," Frankie said trying to be professional.

"No problem," said Olivia smiling back. She could see that something was going on between Frankie and the woman that just walked in and she noticed how tense Desi had become.

As they walked away Desi realized she was staring a hole through Laura's back and snapped out of it. "Sorry about that," she said to Olivia and Sofia.

"That was tense," said Sofia. "I don't think you like her much."

"Not one of my favorite people," Desi said, taking a deep breath. "That was unprofessional of me, I'm so sorry. Please, let me show you our workout room. And don't think our gym is full of drama because that couldn't be further from the truth."

"Drama can be fun," Sofia said thinking she liked this place.

They looked around the workout room that had mirrors on one wall and equipment on the other. There were spin bikes, weighted balls, jump ropes, foam rollers, and just about any kind of equipment to customize a workout.

As they walked out of the room Desi explained there was another workout space just like it across a hallway that led to the back of the building. When they entered the hallway Frankie caught up with them.

"Do you have any questions? Did Desi explain all the classes and extra equipment in the room?" she asked hurriedly.

"She did," Olivia said, turning around, their eyes meeting. Frankie's green eyes showed a flicker of pain and just as quickly it was gone. Olivia felt the strongest urge to reach out and take her hand but, the moment passed.

As they made their way down the hall, she pointed out the restrooms and dressing rooms. "We'll stop in the dressing room on our way back to the front but I wanted to show you the gym first," she said, walking through double doors and holding them open.

They walked into a gym with basketball hoops and volleyball nets. The court was split so one end was for volleyball and the other for basketball.

"We have a volleyball league and a basketball league at different times during the year. Right now it's set up for both games but we can have two volleyball games or two basketball games going at the same time. You're welcome to shoot baskets or work on volleyball skills when there isn't a game going on," explained Frankie.

"Wow, this is nice! I didn't expect there to be a gym," said Sofia. "Why do they call workout places gyms anyway?"

"Great question that I don't really have an answer to," said Desi. "It seems that fitness centers, health clubs, and gyms are synonymous."

"I think I call it a gym because that's where I started. When I was a kid, we went to the gym to play volleyball and basketball indoors," said Frankie.

"Me too," added Olivia.

"Did you play sports?" asked Frankie.

"Yeah, I did in high school but, I haven't in years."

"I think that's why we have the leagues because Frankie and I still like to play games and you have to have people to make up a team," Desi said.

"Maybe you'll get back into it and play with us," Frankie said to Olivia.

"Oh, I don't know about that. I've got to get some of this weight off before I can even think about that," Olivia answered.

"I keep telling her she looks fine," said Sofia.

Frankie smiled and said, "There are lots of reasons to work out and losing weight is certainly one of them but, I like to look at it in a different way."

"What do you mean?" asked Olivia.

"Exercising has been proven not only to improve physical health but, it also improves mental and emotional health. You hear a lot about self-care these days and I think exercising should be included in that. I want a workout to be joyful. Don't get me wrong, it is work, but after just a few minutes your mood will elevate," explained Frankie.

"Wow, you're passionate about this," said Sofia.

"I know. Sometimes I can get a little carried away but, I want you to get all you can out of every class. I want you to have that joy," said Frankie, eyes sparkling.

Olivia was mesmerized by how passionately Frankie spoke. It made her want to join the gym and start her first workout but, it also made her want to get to know Frankie better. Those green eyes were so bright when she was speaking that way Olivia got lost in them.

"Oh, I forgot to mention that we have training plans too. We can train you one-on-one after identifying your goals or we can make a training plan for you to do on your own. There is always someone here to answer questions or assist you with equipment or whatever you need," said Frankie.

Olivia glared at Sofia before she could whisper something else.

Instead, Sofia looked at Frankie then Desi and said, "Wow, you've convinced me and I wasn't planning on joining."

"You weren't?" Frankie said looking at Sofia confused.

"No, I'm here to support my best friend."

"Oh, I get it. I don't like to go into places by myself for the first time either. We want you to feel comfortable and safe. I'll give you my number so the next time you're by yourself, text me and I'll come out and walk in with you," Frankie said with the kindest eyes looking directly at Olivia.

Olivia smiled nodding her head, "I do feel comfortable."

"Let's go back up to the front so we can show you the recovery area," said Desi. "That's really just a fitness term for a place to sit, relax, and have something to drink or a cup of coffee."

On the walk back to the front Olivia took a minute to walk through the different areas again while Sofia and Desi went to the drink area. Frankie stayed with her and gave her space to look around.

"Are there any questions I could answer for you?" Frankie asked.

"Do you teach classes?"

"I do. Desi, Stella, and I own Your Way. You haven't met Stella yet but, you will. We can teach every class we offer. There are some that I'm better at than others but, we believe it's important that we all can step in wherever needed. Natalie is our other instructor that takes care of interns that we have from time to time."

"Do you teach the one-on-one sessions, too?"

"Yes, we all do that too. Are there any classes that you're interested in or did a training plan appeal to you?" As they walked Frankie realized that there was something about Olivia that made her hope she would join the gym. It was her eyes, she could see the kindness in them and they were the most beautiful brown eyes she'd ever seen. Not just brown, but soft and warm and welcoming.

"I don't want to appear pushy. I want you to know everything about us and that there's a place for you here. Oh man, that didn't sound creepy, did it?" Frankie said cringing.

Olivia laughed, "No, that didn't sound creepy and you haven't been pushy. I can tell that you really love this place and what you do and want your members to, also."

"That's true."

"Why don't we go have one of your fancy recovery drinks and you can tell me about your different membership plans," Olivia said smiling. She did feel comfortable here and hoped she'd gain more than just good health from Frankie.

Get The Your Way Series

Printed in Great Britain
by Amazon